Interlude:
A Series of Shorts

M.R. ANGLIN

ACKNOWLEDGMENTS

Thanks to Tazia Hall for the amazing cover.

CONTENTS

THE MEETING ... 7

KAY'S CATERING SERVICE ... 18

TRUST AND BETRAYAL ... 26

CONVERSATING ... 37

MY LITTLE HEROINE ... 42

TYING UP LOOSE ENDS ... 50

GOOD FOR THE SOUL ... 67

BREAKOUT ... 76

ABOUT THE AUTHOR ... 81

THE MEETING

The alarm had a death wish. J.R. was certain of it. It must have if it kept rattling and wailing after the many mornings J.R. had throttled it. This morning, its wish must have been stronger than ever—it kept blaring even after J.R. had pounded on button after button.

J.R. opened his eyes a slit. His sharp ears fell back until they lay flat on his head. With something close to a bark, he caught its cord and yanked it out of the outlet. The alarm clattered to the floor and fell in silent defeat.

But it had left one last revenge: J.R. was awake. He snorted and rolled into a seated position on the king-sized bed. The pristine white walls and rug stood in sharp contrast with the dirty clothes and shoes all over the floor. If his parents had been alive to see this, they would have had a fit. J.R. smirked. So maybe he did win after all.

He yawned and took a deep breath of tropical air. The smell of sand, ocean, and tropical fruit . . . mangoes, maybe ? . . . flowed deep into his nostrils, settling the fur that had risen on the back of his neck. This was the last morning he'd have to wake up early; the last morning he'd have to battle the alarm.

He stretched and rubbed his hand in his armpit. He sniffed it. Though he detected a twinge of body odor, he felt that a heavy dose of deodorant would take care of it. Who needed a shower, anyway? The water always took too long to heat up, and the soap here smelled like a perfumer's overzealous interpretation of flowers. He slipped on some pants and a shirt he found on the floor and stumbled into the family room, rubbing his eyes.

Every window in the house had been opened, letting in the roar of the ocean's tide. Just a few miles down the road, the beach stretched in both directions. A constant breeze blew through the house. That, along with the ceiling fans constantly twirling, kept the house cool in otherwise sweltering conditions. No air conditioning required.

J.R. glanced around the house he had grown up in—white walls, open concept area, lots of windows, and white wicker furniture—everything had its place and everything was clean and polished. He raised the corner of his lip to expose a fang. It was all too open and bright and clean for him. He preferred the closeness and dark wood of his cabin-style house in Justin's Ridge.

"Good morning, J.R." Karalaina, a vixen with salmon colored fur, stood in the kitchen in front of the stove. All four burners glowed red and each pot let out a different smell that mingled together in a delightful fog. She had ears that must have been the size of her head, wavy blonde hair that turned red at the ends, and a curvaceous body. But no matter how beautiful she was or how hard he tried, J.R. could never picture them together in any capacity. It always made him balk.

Karalaina hailed from a country called Expermia and wore a traditional Expermian outfit—a dress with high splits on either side of it and form-fitting pants underneath. Two pieces of cloth hung around her waist, held in place by large, silver pins.

"You're up early again today." Karalaina smiled at him over her shoulder. "Hungry?"

"I'll eat later. Chloe's coming over. After she leaves, I'm going back to bed." J.R. dumped himself in a chair around the breakfast table separating the kitchen from the family room. The place had been set for four people.

He groaned and rested his head on the table. The thought of seeing Chloe left him feeling drained.

"That's right!" Karalaina stirred the contents of a pot. "Xenatha and Katheraine are finally going to meet the woman you've been sneaking off to meet every morning. This will be interesting."

"You make it sound like I'm having some illicit affair." J.R. rested his chin on the table. Not that J.R. minded an illicit affair. But he didn't feel like bantering today. And he didn't feel like explaining why there couldn't be anything at all between him and Chloe. Karalaina would find that out soon enough.

The doorbell chimed.

"That must be her." J.R. hefted himself out of the chair. "Be nice, okay?"

Karalaina tossed a smirk over her shoulder. "I'm always nice."

J.R. rolled his eyes and scratched his hair as he walked to the front door. A twinge of odor came to his nose. Uh, oh! He had forgotten the deodorant. He paused for a moment and considered going to put some on but then shrugged. It was only Chloe. Since when did he ever feel the need to impress her?

He stopped at the stairs that faced the door. From there he saw the upstairs hall and the doors leading to two bedrooms and a bathroom. "Xena! Kathra! Come down here. There's someone I want you to meet."

"Be down in a second, Daddy." Xena's voice lilted down the stairs.

Hearing that voice call him 'Daddy' always put a smile on his face. But once he turned to the front door, the smile left him. He had to take a moment to brace himself before opening it.

A wolf with brown fur the same shade as J.R.'s stood at the front door. She was in her early forties, but her careful make-up and her tailored business suit gave her a younger, yet professional appearance. Her hair—probably dyed to hide the grays—had been pulled back into a tight bun, but a few strands hung loose around her face in order to provide an air of whimsy. An earpiece connected to her cell phone fitted in her right ear. When the door opened, she held up a finger at him. Her hazel eyes were narrowed.

"That place had better be perfect." Chloe put her weight on one foot as she spoke. "This is a very important affair . . . I'll get another caterer. You worry about making that banquet hall look perfect." She pushed a button on her cell phone and turned her attention to J.R. "About time you answered the door. I had an entire conversation while I was waiting."

"Clearly not an entire one, Clo." J.R. crossed his arms.

"It's Chlo*e*, J.R." She shoved past him into the house. "I think you can handle one more syllable."

J.R. leaned out of the house, looking down the walkway. The sun shone on the concrete path and on the fruit trees in the front yard. "Where's Omar?"

"Busy." Chloe straightened her suit. "He got called into the hospital. Never mind that I'm busy, and I made time for this. I swear I do everything in this family." She marched into the kitchen.

J.R. stifled a groan and followed her.

"Good morning." Karalaina greeted Chloe with that annoying, perfect smile of hers. "You must be Chloe. J.R. has told me so much about you."

But Chloe wasn't one to fall for the perfect homemaker act—or any act at all. She studied Karalaina from head to toe. "You must be Karalaina." Chloe didn't sound impressed. "My, you're gorgeous. But I shouldn't be surprised. It would take someone like you to make J.R. settle down. I suppose I can thank you for that."

J.R. froze mid-step. "Eh?"

Karalaina moved her head in a way that made her hair bounce. "We're not dating."

"Never!" J.R. plopped back in his seat.

"I'm sure J.R. has told you about how he found Xenatha and Katheraine in the middle of Jelu." Karalaina turned her back on them to stir a pot.

"Yes, Yes." Chloe dusted the chair before sitting at the table. "He also told me about how after ten years you have returned to claim them." She laced her fingers as she studied Karalaina. "He told me everything; I just don't believe him. He's not exactly trustworthy."

"He's proven very reliable to me." Karalaina removed a plate from the cupboard. "Would you like some breakfast, Chloe?"

"Don't feed her." J.R. twitched his whiskers. "She'll never leave."

Chloe elbowed him, right in the gut. "Thank you, Karalaina. I would love some."

J.R. gasped down air and rubbed his stomach. A grin came to his lips. He had forgotten how tough Chloe was.

Karalaina dished out some eggs, a dish made with cut-up

sausage in a cream sauce, Expermian rice pudding she always made to go with eggs, and toast on the plate before setting it before Chloe. The scent from that plate tickled J.R.'s nose and made his mouth water.

"I must say, J.R." Chloe lifted her chin at him. "For someone who needs my help—and for whom I've carved a lot of time out of my busy schedule—you sure are obnoxious."

"And you act as if we're not family—"

"Don't you dare try to turn this on me, J.R.!" Chloe slapped her hand on the table. "You're the one who got it into his head to be the world's greatest criminal. Whatever happened to you is your own fault, not mine."

"Of course it's my fault!" J.R. threw his hands into the air. "Every little thing that inconveniences your precious clients is my fault. As long as they have money, you care about them more than your own brother!"

Karalaina halted. "Brother?"

"Money has nothing to do with it!" Chloe's nose flared as it did whenever she got angry. "I've worked hard to make sure that anyone who visits the beautiful Isle de Losierres does not get bothered by anyone . . . not the paparazzi, and certainly not lowlifes like you! To that end, I've made this a completely secure island. No unauthorized weapons, cameras, recording devices, image-generators, and NO criminals. My name is trusted all over the world. If anyone found out I so much as let you set foot on my island, they'd lose faith in me. So don't you take this all so flippantly, Justin!"

"Justin?" A white fox kit, eleven years old, appeared. "Your name is Justin, Daddy?" Even though she was only eleven, she already started to develop Karalaina's signature curves. The only difference was her rounded stomach. It made her look like the little girl J.R. hoped she'd stay.

J.R. let his ears fall back. "Never speak that name again."

"You must be Kathra." Chloe extended her hand to her. "What a pretty, little girl you are!"

Kathra's ears fell. She clutched J.R.'s hand and scooted behind him. Chloe's eyebrow rose.

"She's nervous around strangers." J.R. patted Kathra's back. "It's okay, Kitten. Say hi."

"Hi." Kathra put her nose on his arm. She recoiled. "Ew,

Daddy! You didn't take a shower this morning, did you?"

"A straight shooter." Chloe chuckled. "I like that."

J.R. almost let himself smile. When Chloe laughed, he remembered how much he liked her before she grew up into a business woman.

Chloe loaded a fork with the food Karalaina had set out for her. "Xena is coming down, correct?"

"Eventually." J.R. cupped a hand to his mouth. "Xena, get down here!"

"What's taking her so long?" Karalaina placed a plate down for Kathra. "She doesn't usually take this long to get ready."

"She's on the phone with her friend, Mira." Kathra kept her eye on Chloe.

"Mira, huh?" Chloe placed the fork into her mouth. Her eyes widened. "Karalaina, this is delicious! J.R. never mentioned what a good cook you are!"

"With good reason." J.R. pinched Chloe's side. "You have a hard time saying no."

"Things aren't looking for you, Justin Dunsworth." Chloe flared her nose, but her eyes were smiling.

Kathra snickered. "Justin."

"Okay, Chloe. Okay." J.R. ducked his head, but his grin widened. "But remember I have dirt on you too."

Chloe gave him a smirk. "Keep it up, and I'll tell her what the 'R' stands for."

J.R. clamped his mouth shut.

"Karalaina, have you ever thought of catering?" Chloe put more food in her mouth. "I have an event in two weeks, and my normal caterer can't make it. It's put me in a bind. You'd be perfect to fill in."

"Thank you, but no." Karalaina motioned to J.R. and Kathra. "With two kids and J.R., I'm too busy around here. Family first, I always say."

"Karie, I think this is something you should consider." J.R. rested his arms on the table. "It might be good for you to get out of the house every once in a while."

Karalaina turned her back on him. "Like I said, I don't have time."

"Karalaina . . ."

Karalaina ears fell flat. "I said no!"

The house plunged into silence. Karalaina picked up her ears and busied herself by turning all the burners on low.

"I'll leave my card if you change your mind." Chloe removed a card from her front jacket pocket and handed it to Karalaina.

"Thank you." Karalaina dropped the card on the counter without a second look.

Silence again invaded the kitchen. Kathra clutched to J.R., and Karalaina kept her back to him. His fur stood on end. He could face all sorts of dangers—police shootouts, high stake robberies gone wrong, knife fights—but he could never stand to be in the vicinity of an angry woman.

"Everybody looks so serious." Xena's voice cut through the tension, settling J.R.'s nerves. He felt as if he could breathe again.

"Morning, Kid," he said.

"Good morning, Daddy." Xena, a fox kit—or rather a vixen, as J.R. had to keep reminding himself—kissed his cheek. Her fur looked shiny gray, and she had pulled back her hair in her usual messy ponytail. She wore a full black swimsuit that somehow gave her slender figure some shape and a black and gold wrap around her waist. "Morning, Mom."

"Good morning, Xenatha," Karalaina said without turning.

"What's with you?" Xena put her hand on a hip. "Did Daddy say something to upset you again?"

Karalaina chuckled. When she turned, she had a real smile on her face. "I'm fine."

"Kat, stop clinging on Daddy like that." Xena put her arm around Kathra's shoulder. "Come. Sit down and eat. We have to go soon."

Kathra, ears down, sat in a chair beside J.R. She picked up her fork and started eating.

Chloe had been watching her without a word. "You certainly have a handle on how to run this house."

"Um, thanks." Xena glanced at J.R. while trying to look like she wasn't.

"Would you like to introduce me, J.R.?" Chloe pressed her lips together.

"I'm getting to it. Keep your shirt on. Please." J.R. took Xena's hand. "Xena, this is Chloe."

Xena's eyes landed on Chloe. They traced her up and down

much the same way Chloe had examined Karalaina earlier. "Good morning, Miss Chloe. My name's Xena."

"So I've gathered." Chloe stood. "Would you mind turning around please?"

Xena let one of her ears flatten. "Why?"

"It's okay, Kid. Do it." J.R. chewed the inside of his cheek. He knew what Chloe was searching for. Last night he had secretly changed all the settings on Xena's image-generator—enough that her fur seemed abnormally shiny, but not enough to cause alarms for someone who didn't know what they were looking for. Hopefully, he'd done enough.

"Well, that was interesting." Chloe dabbed her lips with a napkin. "Shiny, gray fur. It's rare, but I don't see what all the fuss is about. Think about my offer, Karalaina. The rest of you need to vacate this premises by tomorrow morning."

"You mean we can't stay here?" Xena's mouth dropped open. "Daddy, why?"

He hadn't done enough. J.R.'s stomach heaved as if Chloe had elbowed him again. "Come on, Clo. They're children."

"Maybe I didn't make myself clear, J.R." Chloe thrust her face in his. "I don't care if you are my little brother. You chose the life you lead, and I'm not letting your problem become my emergency. I will do anything it takes to make sure no degenerates like you get on this island."

Xena marched in between them, her fur rising. "Don't say that about him! He's not a degenerate! You don't know anything about him."

"Kid . . ."

Chloe's nose flared. "I know plenty about him."

"No, you don't!" Xena clenched her fists. "If you did, you won't say those things!"

"What did I expect?" Chloe swung around to the door. "You're probably as much of a reprobate as he is."

"Now wait a minute, Chloe." J.R. caught her shoulder. "You can't say that. The Kid is as good as they come."

"Says the one who crashed King Maximilian's wedding and then left a suspicious package in his bedroom that got the entire palace evacuated." Chloe put her hands on her hips. "So how about it, little, good girl? Are you proud of your 'daddy' and his $6 million bounty?”

"Chloe, that's enough!" J.R. shoved her away from Xena. "You have no business—"

"I know the things he's done." Xena's voice was soft, barely audible over the shouting. Yet somehow it cut through it all. "I know he's a criminal, and I know what he's done is wrong." She played with her fingers as her eyes shone with tears. "But he's my dad just the same. I don't know what I'd do if the police really did come and take him away from me. Every time I hear a siren, I jump . . . I . . . I . . ." She wiped her eyes.

J.R.'s heart dropped. He had no idea she felt this way. "Oh, Kid." He put an arm around her.

Chloe gazed at them with her mouth slightly open. But then her eyes hardened, and her ears stood straight. "Really heartbreaking, J.R. Did you have her rehearsing that all night?"

"Chloe—"

"Do you really expect me to believe that King Maximilian, the most powerful ruler in the entire world, is after you because of her, a vixen with gray fur? Need I remind you that his wife is also a gray-furred vixen?" Chloe glared at him, her eyes seemingly on fire. "You know, I almost believed you, J.R. As fantastic as your story was, the way you spoke almost got me. But you telling the truth . . . what a joke!" She swung around to the door.

J.R. let his eyes drop to the floor. He couldn't bring himself to look at Xena or Kathra or even Karalaina. They were all counting on him to keep them safe. He had to think of something fast.

"Chloe, wait!" J.R. caught her arm. "At least let me leave them with Karalaina while I go. I'll send for them once I figure something out."

"Daddy, no!" Xena's voice rose to nearly a screech. "You said you wouldn't leave me. You promised!" She clutched his shirt, her eyes wild with fear.

"But . . . but . . ." J.R. cursed inside. He had no other options.

"I have to leave." Chloe shook off his grip.

J.R. squeezed his eyes shut. "I'll tell you the truth, Chloe."

Chloe crossed her arms and glared at him though narrowed eyes.

He paused a moment to review his options, but Chloe left him no other choice. "Turn off the image-generator, Kid."

The color drained from Xena's face. It was visible even

underneath her image-generated fur.

"Image-generator?" Chloe snarled. "I do not believe you, J.R. I do not allow image-generators on this island! No exceptions. How could you—"

J.R. bared his teeth at her. "Chloe, stuff it!"

Chloe rumbled deep in her throat but quieted.

"Go on, Kid." J.R. patted Xena's shoulder. "It's okay."

Xena's eyes moistened. She pulled the hair tie she kept her image-generator hidden in out of her hair. The moment she turned it off, her fur morphed into bright silver that reflected the white of the walls and the green of the trees outside. But the real change rested in Xena. She slumped her shoulders, and her eyes never left the floor. J.R. felt a lump rise in his throat as all her self-confidence drained away.

But Chloe didn't notice past the fur. "Oh, my. That is . . . I . . . well . . ."

"It's a genetic disorder that causes her to store metals in her fur." J.R. rested his hand on top of Xena's head. She looked up at him with the most pitiful expression. "It makes her a target. Now do you see why I need to hide out here?"

Chloe pressed her lips together the way she did when deep in thought. It reminded J.R. of his mother. "This changes things." She swung around to the door. "I'll talk to Omar."

"Does this mean we can stay?"

"It means I'll talk to Omar about it." Chloe opened the door.

"You don't leave until I get a clear answer." J.R. pushed the door closed. "We both know that you're the one who always makes all the decisions."

"Let me go, J.R. I have meetings." Chloe tried to pull open the door, but as tough as she was, J.R. was tougher.

"Answer me first." J.R. examined his nails. "I can stand here all day, Clo."

Chloe glowered at him. "Justin Richards Dunsworth, you let go of the door this instant!"

J.R. stiffened. Silence descended on the whole house. He glanced behind him. Xena lifted up her eyes and burst into snickers.

"Justin *Richards*?" Kathra burst into laughter. Even Karalaina covered her mouth with her hands to hide her chuckles.

J.R. turned to Chloe. See if she was going to leave now. But when he focused on her, she was smirking.

"Better get used to it if you're going to stay," she said.

"You mean it?"

"I have to go, J.R." Chloe pulled on the door.

J.R. released it. "Thanks, Chloe. It goes without saying that no one is to know about Xena's fur."

"Who are you talking to about keeping secrets?" Chloe motioned around her. "This is the Isle de Losierres, the place where secrets come to die. But I will tell you this, if you do anything to hurt my reputation . . . if you so much as pick up one cent that doesn't belong to you . . . then you and your brood will be off this island so fast, your tails will be in your ears! Got it?"

"That's fair." J.R. leaned on the doorway. "Tell you what: I'll even put my skills to work for you."

"I don't want you to—"

"I'll give you a monthly report on everywhere your security is lacking." J.R. gave a toothy grin. "Think of it as payment in lieu of rent."

Chloe narrowed her eyes at him. "My security is not lacking."

"Oh, yeah?" J.R. picked up a bag by the door. "Then how'd I get three image-generators, a working camera, and a laser pistol on the Isle?"

Chloe peeked inside the bag. "A gun, a camera, and *three* image-generators?"

"More like five." J.R. scratched his chin. "And that's the truth, I swear."

Chloe pressed her lips together and stared at him.

J.R. shrugged. "Gotta have backups for the Kid."

"Fine." Chloe snatched the bag. "Have the reports on my desk by the first of each month." She marched out of the door. "And one more thing." Chloe smiled at him. "I'm glad you're home."

J.R. grinned. In a way, he was too.

KAY'S CATERING SERVICE

"Justin Richards!" Xenatha snickered.

Karalaina glanced over her shoulder when J.R. and Xenatha re-entered the kitchen. Xenatha laughed so hard her cheeks turned red.

"I can't believe *that's* what 'J.R.' stands for." Katheraine banged her fists on the table.

Karalaina placed both hands on her chest. It warmed her heart to see them laugh like that. She spent years dreaming about reuniting with her children, and to see them laugh like that . . . her heart soared out of her chest. She'd never let anything tear her away from them again.

J.R. plopped himself down in his chair. "I'll never forgive my parents for naming me that."

"I can see why you go with 'J.R.'" Karalaina grinned at him over her shoulder. "Justin Richards doesn't have that edge."

"Funny." J.R. snorted.

"So . . . why did we have to get permission to stay from that woman?" Xenatha pulled her hair back into a ponytail and activated the image-generator. Her fur changed back to gray. Karalaina didn't much like the change, but they had to keep her fur hidden. If anyone found out about her ability to manipulate electricity, she and her girls could be separated all over again.

"My parents were real-estate moguls and had properties all over the place." J.R. scratched his head. "When they died, the will stipulated that most of the property be sold and the money split between the three of us and some other charities and stuff, but it also specifically stated that Chloe and Omar were to get control of this place and I was to get Justin's Ridge. They asked that we never sell those properties."

"Why would you ever want to sell Justin's Ridge, anyway?" Xenatha sat down beside him.

J.R. shrugged. "Beats me."

"It is strange, though." Karalaina leaned on the kitchen counter. "Why would real-estate moguls care so much about you keeping Justin's Ridge? It's not exactly a tourist spot."

"I think my dad grew up there or something. I used to visit every summer till my parents finally shipped me off to live there. Couldn't handle me, I guess." J.R. picked up his fork. "Where's the grub?"

"Coming up." Karalaina turned back to the stove.

"I can get it." Xenatha stood to her feet.

"No, no. Sit, sweetie," Karalaina said over her shoulder. Xenatha sank back in her chair. Her ears fell a bit.

"So, let me get something straight." Katheraine shoveled food in her mouth. Now that Chloe had left her appetite seemed to return. "Is Chloe your sister, Daddy?"

J.R. nodded. "And Omar's my brother."

"That means we have an auntie." Katheraine clapped her hands. "And an uncle."

Xenatha bounced in her chair. "I've always wanted an aunt."

"You had an aunt, you know, and her name was Rose!" Karalaina slammed her hands on the counter. "How could you forget her after all she did for you?" The words exploded out of her mouth before she could stop herself.

Xenatha's ears lowered. She turned her eyes to the kitchen table. "Sorry, Mom."

"Yeah. Sorry." Katheraine shifted in her chair.

Karalaina winced. She could have kicked herself. She knew they didn't mean anything by it. Rose died in the Jelu Tragedy years ago—Xenatha and Katheraine couldn't possibly remember her. But Karalaina couldn't stand the thought of that dear women ever being forgotten.

"I'm going to go upstairs and finish getting ready." Katheraine scampered out of her chair.

"Don't take all day." Xenatha turned in her chair to watch her. "I'm not waiting for you much longer." When she turned to sit properly in her chair, her eyes fell on J.R.'s empty mug. Her ears pricked up. "Daddy, you don't have any coffee. I'll get it." She hopped to her feet.

"Don't bother yourself, sweetie. I think I finally got it right." For weeks Karalaina had been trying to replicate the way Xenatha made J.R.'s coffee, but it never turned out quite right.

"Karalaina . . ." J.R. said.

"Yes?" Karalaina turned in time to see Xenatha touch J.R.'s arm. She shook her head and sunk in her chair, ears fallen.

"What is it, J.R.?" Karalaina set the mug in front of him.

"Never mind." J.R. tapped his finger on the mug's handle.

"Okay, then." Karalaina smoothed down Xenatha's unruly hair. "You're not eating, sweetie?"

Xenatha shook her head. "I'm not hungry."

"Then what do you have planned today?" Karalaina sat in the chair next to Xenatha.

"I'm going to meet Mira at the beach." Xenatha let her gaze fall on the counter. She didn't look at Karalaina.

"The beach . . ." Karalaina let her ears angle back. "Is that a good idea."

"She's right." J.R. turned to Xenatha. "I mean, salt water is conductive, and . . ."

"Don't worry about it, Daddy. Hunter says that the ocean is so big that the electricity conducted over my fur won't matter much. But on the safe side, he says that I should stay 15 feet away from people when I'm in the water. That sort of defeats the purpose, so I'm not going in." Xenatha held her hands between her knees. "Plus I think he kind of pulled that number from the air."

J.R. nodded. Karalaina, too, felt her nerves about the situation ebb. In addition to being Xenatha's suitor, Hunter had the honor of being the only Silver Fox Trainer in the world. He taught Xenatha how to keep her electricity in check. If he cleared her to go to the beach, it should be fine.

"It's too bad, though, Xenatha." Karalaina tilted her head slightly. "You like to swim, don't you? I hope this won't ruin your fun."

"It won't." Xenatha tapped her hands on the table.

"Then what are you going to do?" J.R. said.

"Mira's going to show me around and introduce me to all her friends." Xenatha balled up her fists. "I'm so excited, Daddy. Things have been great since Mira came up to the house to introduce herself. No one here knows what a freak I am. It's like I get to start over."

Karalaina furrowed her brows. "You're not a freak, Xenatha."

"I know." Xenatha tapped her sandaled feet on the floor.

"Don't get caught up in the stuff that's happened to you lately, Kid." J.R. ruffled her hair. "You show them all what a great girl you are."

Xenatha shoved J.R.'s hand off her head. "You're only saying that because I'm your daughter."

"That and because it's true." J.R. tugged on her ear.

Xenatha threw her arms around his neck. "I love you, Daddy."

Karalaina watched them a moment. She stood, picked up a kitchen towel, and started wiping the counter, not because it needed wiping but because she needed to do something with her hands to keep herself from crying. No matter how hard she tried, Xenatha seemed to prefer J.R. to her. She opened up to him in a way she never did with Karalaina.

The telephone rang once then stopped.

"Oh, great." Xenatha threw her head back. "That means Kathra got it. Now she'll never be ready."

"Xena!" Katheraine called from upstairs. "Phone. It's Hunter!"

Xenatha shot out of her chair. "I'll take it upstairs."

"Why can't you take it down here?" J.R. narrowed his eyes.

"Daddy!" Xenatha shook her head before dashing upstairs.

"You're too overprotective, J.R." Karalaina forced herself to smile. She'd never admit to him that Xenatha liked him better. "Of course she'll want some privacy when she talks to him."

"I'm glad she went upstairs. I just wish it hadn't been to talk to that punk." J.R. fingered the fur on his chin. "I wanted to talk to you."

"What about?"

"You should reconsider about the catering thing, Karie."

"I told you, J.R. I'm not interested."

"Karie . . ."

Karalaina threw the kitchen towel down. "You do not have a monopoly on those girls. I want a chance to get to know them, too! How am I going to do that if I'm out of the house?"

"I promised Xena I wouldn't say anything, but I'm sick of seeing her like this." J.R. gripped his mug. "You're invading her space. That cooking and cleaning stuff is Xena's thing. She was all about it until you came along and stole it from her."

"Xenatha is too young for so much responsibility." Karalaina glanced around. Now where did she leave that broom? "She's just a teenager."

"You're not listening, Karalaina." J.R. banged the table with his fist, causing all the dishes to rattle. "You're making Xena feel pushed aside. Think about what she's going through—"

"You don't know what you're talking about, J.R.!"

"I do know because Xena tells me these things. She talks to me, Karalaina. When was the last time you had a conversation with her?"

Karalaina gaped at him. Was it that obvious?

"Look." J.R. lowered his voice. "You can't go back to the way things were when you left them. They've changed."

"Oh, shut up and drink your coffee." Karalaina turned her back on him.

"It doesn't taste right."

"You didn't even try it."

"I don't have to." J.R. swatted the mug, tipping it over.

Karalaina put her hand on her hip. "I am not cleaning that up."

"Good! It's about time!"

Karalaina snorted and turned her back on him once again.

"Daddy, what happened to your coffee?" Xenatha walked into the kitchen.

"I knocked it over," J.R. said. Karalaina could almost feel him glaring at her.

Karalaina peeked over her shoulder. Xenatha grabbed a sponge from the sink.

"So you couldn't clean up your mess?" Xenatha wiped up the coffee and picked up his mug. Though she scolded him, her eyes shone.

Karalaina let her gaze fall on the coffeepot. Maybe . . . maybe J.R. was right. Well, one way to find out. She poured some more coffee in a clean mug and handed it to Xenatha as she passed.

"Perhaps you can make it the way he likes it."

A smile lit up Xenatha's face. "Thanks, Mom."

"You're welcome." Karalaina gazed at Xenatha. The change in her attitude lit up the kitchen as she fixed J.R.'s coffee. Even her shoulders seemed to relax as if some tension had been released.

"Here, Daddy." Xenatha set the coffee in front of J.R.

"Thanks, Kid." J.R. gave Karalaina a look.

Karalaina shook out the kitchen towel and turned up her nose. A coincidence . . . simply a coincidence. What did he know, anyway?

"What did Hunter want?" J.R. sipped his coffee.

"He wanted to take me out today." Xenatha caught the end of her ponytail. "But I already made plans with Mira, so . . ." She twirled her fingers in her hair.

"Something wrong, Xenatha?" Karalaina turned to her.

Xenatha opened her mouth to say something but instead shook her head. "No; it's nothing." She turned to the stairs. "Kathra, come on!"

Karalaina turned to hang the towel in his place. J.R. *was* wrong. Xenatha just didn't want to open up to her. But then again . . . Karalaina peeked at Xenatha over her shoulder . . . she did look like she wanted to say something. Maybe a little more effort would get her to open up.

"Coming! Coming!" Kathcraine dashed down the stairs. "I'm ready."

"About time." Xenatha put her hands on her hips.

"Xenatha, before you go, I'd like to talk to you a moment." Karalaina approached her.

"What's wrong?" Xenatha said.

Karalaina played with the fabric on her dress. "Chloe asked me to do some catering for a party in two weeks, and that's a lot of work . . ."

J.R. raised his eyes from his coffee. Karalaina didn't spare him a look.

"If I do it . . . and if I continue to cater after the party. . . I won't be able to keep up with the housework and cooking. So, would you mind picking back up where you left off when I arrived?"

"Sure! And I can help you with the catering, too!" Xenatha halted. "I mean . . . if you want me to."

Karalaina blinked. Was that all it took? "I'd like that, Xenatha. And you can tell me how to make the coffee so J.R. likes it."

"And . . . and . . ." Xenatha fingered the fabric of her wrap. "And . . . I've wanted to ask you if maybe . . . you can teach me how to make a peach pie. Daddy loves them, but I've never been able to make a good one."

J.R. smacked his lips. "But I've enjoyed the attempts."

Katheraine turned up her nose. "I think it needs more nutmeg, but she won't listen to me."

"I'd be happy to help you." Karalaina cocked her head. "Why didn't you ask me before?"

Xenatha dropped her eyes. "I thought if I did, you'd make it for me instead of helping me."

Karalaina blinked. "Oh."

"We have to go." Xenatha gave Karalaina a hug. "Bye, Mom."

"Bye." Katheraine gave her a hug as well.

"Bye, Daddy." Xenatha leaned close to J.R. "I told you it would work out," she whispered.

Karalaina knew that Xenatha hadn't meant for Karalaina to hear her, so she pretended she hadn't. Instead she picked up the card Chloe had left her.

Xenatha and Katheraine clattered out of the house and slammed the door behind them.

"Atta girl, Karie." J.R. sipped his coffee.

"Did you see the way she looked at me when I told her that I wouldn't be cooking anymore?" Karalaina closed her eyes. "I had no idea I was taking so much away from her."

"Of course you knew. You just didn't care." J.R. yawned. "You're a very selfish person, Karalaina—probably the most selfish person I know."

Karalaina gaped.

"But that's okay." J.R. stretched. "That peppy, perfect attitude of yours was getting on my last nerve."

Karalaina laughed to herself.

J.R. sipped his coffee again. "And you finally got this coffee tasting right."

"But I didn't . . ." She paused. "Never mind. I'm glad you're finally happy with it."

"I am." J.R. raised his mug. "Keep this up, and you will get along fine."

Karalaina nodded. She picked up the phone to dial Chloe's number.

25

TRUST AND BETRAYAL

"I swear, Kat, you take the longest time to get ready." Xena pulled out of the driveway in the red hover car she had gotten for her birthday. They didn't need to drive the mile or so to the beach, but Kathra insisted on not getting her hair messy by walking in the wind. And since the drama that surrounded her birthday, Xena didn't mind driving her car as much as she could.

"At least I don't slop all my clothes together as if it didn't matter." Kathra thrust her nose in the air. "If it wasn't for me, you'd be wearing that old, faded green swimming suit you have."

"How could I wear my green suit?" Xena smirked at her sister. "It's back home in Justin's Ridge. We had to leave home without anything, remember?"

"You know what I mean."

Xena glanced down at the black swimsuit she wore. The gold-toned charm that hung from the front caught her eye. It flashed in the sun. "I guess you did do a good job of picking this out."

"And that wrap is too cute!" Kathra tugged at Xena's black wrap printed with gold flowers. "It's too bad that Hunter can't see you. He'd think you were hot."

The blood rushed to Xena's face. Even the thought of Hunter liking her outfit made her want to giggle like an idiot.

"How come you're not hanging out with him today?" Kathra kicked her feet. "You've been so cozy with him these past few weeks that I thought you'd never stay apart."

"He told me last week that he was going to be busy catching up with his job. The Expermian incident kind of put him behind." Xena pulled into the beach parking lot. "But when he called this morning, it was to tell me that he was done early. He wanted to take me out, but I had already made plans." She lowered her ears. "He was so disappointed."

"So?" Kathra pointed. "Xena, there's a parking space!"

Xena pulled into the space. Each beach parking spot had its own canopy designed to keep cars cooler while parked. Boy, the rich had it good.

"You shouldn't feel bad about not being able to go out with him, Xena." Kathra got her beach bag out of the car. "You don't have to drop everything when he calls."

"I know, but I've never had a guy who wanted to be with me like this before. I'm . . . sort of afraid that if I don't go out with when he calls that he'll . . . I don't know . . . he'll get tired of me or something." Xena put her purse in the trunk. "It sounds stupid, huh?"

"I dunno . . ." Kathra cocked her head. "You're not taking your purse?"

"I don't like purses." Xena held up a wallet had a chain on it. "I've got everything I need in here." She hung it around her neck.

"If you say so." Kathra gazed up at the sky. "I don't think Hunter will get tired of you if you don't hang out with him all the time, but I do understand how you feel. You don't want him to meet someone else when you're not around."

Xena winced. "Wow, Kat. That's exactly what I was thinking, but hearing out loud makes it sound pathetic." She took a deep breath. "It's not like I don't trust him—I do, but— oh . . . it's so confusing. I was going to talk to Mom about it, but . . . I don't know . . . I feel weird talking to her."

"Didn't she help you with Hunter before, though?" Kathra held her bag in both hands. "When we were at that fuel station after we fled Expermia."

"Yeah, but . . ." Xena rubbed the back of her neck. "Daddy practically pushed me into telling her what was wrong."

"She's easy to talk to, Xena."

"I know." Xena let her ears tilt back. "Maybe I'll try again once she starts that catering thing. I find it more comfortable to talk while I'm cooking. Meet me back at the car at one o'clock so we can get home in time for lunch."

"Are you cooking today?"

"I don't know. Maybe. I don't know when she'll start that catering thing."

"I hope you do cook." Kathra shut the car door. "I don't want to say anything, but she puts too much salt in my food."

Xena flipped Kathra's braid. "She doesn't know that you're eleven going on forty-two."

"Too much sodium is not good for anyone."

"I'll find a way to let Mom know how you like your food. Now, you're going to be with Khendera, right?"

"We're going to go shopping, hang out at the Burger Shack, and maybe go swimming."

"Don't ruin your lunch, okay?" Xena trotted off. "Call me if you need anything."

"Okay." Kathra waved after her.

Xena waved at her over her shoulder and headed off toward the Boardwalk.

The place the residents of the Isle called the "Boardwalk" referred to an elevated, wooden pier that extended over the ocean on wooden stilts. Restaurants and shops—also built on stilts— stood in the middle of the pier so that it looked like the wooden walkway wrapped around them. Girl and guys . . . most in swim suits and trunks . . . meandered up and down the walk, window shopping or sitting at umbrella-shaded tables at outdoor cafés. Here the scent of the sea mingled with the smell of freshly-popped caramel popcorn.

After going down wooden steps to the beach, a wooden path ran along the edge of the sand, separating the beach from the street. The other side of the road had been built up with more restaurant and shops. Locals called this the "Boulevard." While the Boardwalk had the best souvenir shops and casual dining cafés on the Isle, the Boulevard had some of the most expensive and exclusive restaurants and clothing shops on the Isle—not *the* most expensive, but close.

In either direction, the beach stretched out for miles. The ocean shone a blue so bright, it stung Xena's eyes. Sunbathers lay on the golden sand, and swimmers dotted the ocean with brightly colored swimsuits.

At the base the stairs leading up to the Boardwalk stood a brown wolf wearing a pink and gold bikini top and the shortest jeans shorts that Xena had ever seen. Bronze highlights striped her dark brown hair, and pink flip-flops decorated with white daisies on the tongs adorned her feet.

"Mira!" Xena darted up to her.

"Xena, there you are!" Mira waved her phone in the air. "I was trying to call you."

"Really?" Xena patted her suit and wrap, but of course she had no pockets. "I left my phone in the car."

Mira gaped at her with her eyes wide in horror. "How could you leave your phone anywhere?"

"I'm not used to having one." Xena tucked her hair behind her ears. "My dad handmade these communicators for us that we used to—"

"Homemade communi . . ." Mira raised the corner of her lip, exposing one of her surprisingly sharp teeth. "Stop. Please, just stop." She grunted in disgust. "I am so going to have a chat with that father of yours."

Xena snickered. Ever since she and Mira first met, Mira had a command over J.R. that Xena had only seen in Melody.

"I can't wait for you to meet all my friends." Mira pulled Xena along. "It's hard to meet someone who's not seriously stuck on themselves on the Isle. I was so glad when Mama called and told me you were staying—"

"What does your mom know about that?"

"She met you this morning . . . or at least that's what she said. She met with you, Kathra, Karalaina, and Uncle J.R."

"So wait! Your mom's Chloe?" Xena squealed. "That means we're cousins!"

"I know; isn't that great?" Mira bounced on her tip-toes. "When Mama told me you were staying, I literally screamed. I've always wanted a sister or cousins, but Mama's not going to have any more children and Uncle Omar isn't getting married anytime soon. He doesn't have time for a relationship. Mama says his only love is his job. And we never thought Uncle J.R. would settle down."

"Wow. You're my cousin." Xena grinned so wide she squinted. "I wish they would have told me about it."

Mira let go of Xena's hand. "Mama doesn't have a very high opinion of J.R. Dunsworth."

Xena rolled her eyes. "So I've noticed."

"Oh, look! There are my friends." Mira waved. "Hi, girls!"

A chameleon, a raccoon, and a tigress waved back to Mira. They all sat under an umbrella at an outdoor café and sipping colored drinks with umbrellas in them. The table stood next to the Boardwalk's railing and overlooked the beach below.

"Guys, this is Xena, the one I've been telling you about." Mira sat at the table. "Xena, this is Katydee, but we call her Katie."

"Hi." The raccoon waved her fingers. Her poofy, brown hair had been pulled half up in a ponytail but the back rested on her shoulders. Xena blinked at all that hair. That must be what the shampoo commercials meant by "voluptuous volume."

Mira turned to the chameleon. "This is Dorina, but we call her Dori."

"Hello." Dori turned a warm shade of yellow that made Xena feel like she stood in the sun—which she was.

Mira motioned to the tigress. "And this is Shandra."

"That's Shandra. Not Shandee or Shan. Shandra." She held out her hand to Xen as if she wanted her to kiss it.

Mira rested her cheek on her hands. "She's 'special.'"

"I am." Shandra crinkled her nose as Xena shook her hand.

"Sit down, Xena." Mira patted the seat next to her.

Xena took a deep breath and made sure her electricity stayed level. She had a chance to make friends here . . . real friends. She didn't want to mess it up.

"Xena." Shandra leaned in close to her, her eyes roving around Xena's face. Her lips pressed in a line. "I feel like I know you from somewhere."

Xena leaned back. "We've never met."

"Still." Shandra put her finger under nose. "Are you a celebrity? Have I seen you on TV?"

Xena started. Shandra shouldn't have known Xena's face . . . unless Max had posted her picture somewhere. "No! You've never seen my face. I . . . I mean, you shouldn't have."

"I've never seen her before." Katie sipped her drink. "And my dad would know. He's a private investigator."

Xena stiffened. A private investigator? Someone like that could find out everything about her in seconds. Xena sat still and tried to not look like she needed investigating.

Dori rolled her eyes. "We know what father does, Katie. You

don't have to keep saying it."

Shandra leaned back, her eyes studying Xena. "I know I've seen your face somewhere."

Xena felt her hands tremble and her fur rise. If Shandra and her friends found out about her secret, she and her family would have to leave the Isle and go on the run again. Her chance to start over would be ruined.

"Oh, man! Look, it's him!" Dori stood to her feet, her tail curling. "His Royal Hotness."

"Where?" All the girls turned to look at the beach.

Xena sighed. The appearance of this guy, whoever he was, provided the distraction she needed. Now she'd have to find a way to let J.R. know that her picture had been posted somewhere. Too bad she'd left her phone in the car.

"He is soo fine!" Mira sighed, her tail wagging a bit.

Xena turned her attention to the direction they watched. She spotted a teenage fox spreading a blanket on the beach. His sandy hair faded to a shade of pink or purple at the ends. The sun glinted off the earrings in his ears. After lying on the blanket, he slipped on some sunglasses, scratched his scalp, and lay still.

"That's Hunter, Xena." Mira batted her eyelashes. "Every time he comes here, all the girls go crazy."

"But he never stays long." Dori rested her cheek on her hand. "I wonder what he's doing tonight."

"Going out with me." Shandra smirked. "He just doesn't know it yet."

Xena bit her bottom lip in a vain attempt to stifle the snicker that burst out of her. "Does he know you call him 'His Royal Hotness'?"

"Are you crazy?" Mira swung around to face Xena.

"If he found out we call him that, I'd die." Dori put her hand on her heart. "Unless, you know, he likes it. Then I'd totally tell him it was all my idea."

"You girls are sheep." Shandra clicked her tongue.

Mira put a hand on her hip. "As if you wouldn't go out with him."

"Of course I would; he's hot." Shandra flipped her hair. "But at least I'm not drooling."

Xena chuckled. "I am so going to tell him that you call him that now."

"Do you . . . know him?" Katie gaped at Xena.

"He's . . . he's my boyfriend." Xena felt her face flush.

Katie and Dori glanced at each other and burst into laughter. Mira blinked at her.

But Shandra's mouth dropped open. "No! It can't be!" She whipped out her phone and started swiping the screen. "That's where I know you from!" She held up her phone and inspected it then Xena and then back again.

The girls leaned in to look at what Shandra was going on about.

"No way!" Dori said.

"Whoa!" Katie said.

"What?" Xena took the phone from Shandra's hands. Shandra had brought up Hunter's Circlefriends page, a social media site Xena had heard of before. Hunter had even helped her set up a page of her own. Once set up, a user could invite people to be a part of their "circle of friends." Anyone in the circle could add, post, share, and upload pictures to each other's pages.

Hunter had posted a picture of Xena standing at the ocean's edge with the moon shining above her. He had written the caption, "Dunno what's prettier: the beach or my girl."

"Oh." Xena swiped the phone where another picture of her waited, brought to life by the holographic display of Shandra's phone. This time she stood in a candy shop. "I didn't realize he was posting pictures of our dates." Well, that explained who was posting pictures of her. She only hoped he didn't put any information that could lead anyone to track her. Then again, it was Hunter. He tracked people for a living. He wouldn't do something so stupid.

"So you *are* his girlfriend?" Dori stared at Xena as if she had turned purple.

Xena nodded, allowing Katie to take the phone. "At least, I think I am. One day, he started introducing me to his friends as his girlfriend, so . . ."

"This is not possible!" Shandra shot to her feet. "How does a girl like you land a guy like that?" Her tail had bristled to twice its size.

Xena's ears pricked. "What's that supposed to mean?"

"It means that I'm prettier than you." Shandra put her hands on her hips. "Most of the girls on this beach are prettier than you."

Xena felt her electricity rise. "Th—that doesn't mean anything."

"Careful, Shandra." Mira took a sip of her drink. "Your jealous is showing."

Shandra growled at Mira. "I am not jealous."

"Oh, great," Dori crossed her arms. "There goes Candie."

Xena looked over her shoulder. A white and black Persian cat wearing a swimsuit that Xena could only describe as pieces of clothes held together by strings sashayed up the beach, making a beeline for Hunter. Her tail swished back and forth making every guy she passed stop and turn to stare.

Shandra clenched her fists. "I cannot stand that little tramp!"

"She's had her eye on Hunter for ages." Dori turned a shade of pea green, a sign of disgust, Xena thought.

"If Hunter really is your boyfriend, do something about it." Shandra gave Xena a shove. "Go over there and tell Candie to shove off."

Xena turned to watch Hunter. He lay still, not knowing what loomed toward him. In a few moments, he would be bombarded by a gorgeous face and a curvaceous body; both qualities that Xena lacked.

She started to head toward the Boardwalk stairs, but stopped. What she had said to Kathra came back to her: "It's not like I don't trust him; I do . . ." Well, wasn't trust believing he wouldn't betray her even if she didn't agree to go out with him today?

"Well?" Shandra stood right behind her. "I'll come with you if you're scared."

"I'm not going. Hunter is a guy I know I can trust." Xena returned to her seat and sat down—the hardest decision she ever had to make. "He won't betray me. He won't." She clasped her trembling hands together.

"I wouldn't be so sure about that." Shandra's voice sounded softer than it had been until now.

Xena looked at her and then Hunter. Candie had approached him, but he didn't move until she touched his arm. Then he jumped. He glanced around, removed his shades, and pulled ear buds out of his ears. He ogled her up and down.

"This is disgusting!" Shandra threw herself in her chair. She guzzled her drink with so much fervor she choked on an ice cube.

Mira leaned close to Xena. "Shandra was dating this guy for six months, and Candie broke them up in five minutes. Then she dumped him a week later. She did it because she was mad at

Shandra."

Xena blinked as she watched Candie stroke Hunter's arm. Six months? She and Hunter had only been dating for a few weeks.

But Hunter pulled his arm away from Candie. He said something to her, put his sunglasses back on, and lay back on his blanket. Xena sighed with relief.

"Xena." Shandra had her eyes on the scene. "It's not over yet. Don't get your hopes up. Are you sure you don't want to break this up? I'll come with you and tell her where she can stuff her tail if you want."

Xena bit her lips together. She had to trust Hunter. What kind of relationship . . . or even friendship . . . did they have if she didn't? And if he wasn't trustworthy, wouldn't she want to know it? But that rationalization didn't make her heart stop pounding. He was the first guy who had ever looked at her twice or told her she was pretty. If he betrayed her now, then . . . maybe all those things he said weren't true.

"And here's her finishing move." Dori surged red in anger.

Xena picked up her head. Candie had leaned over Hunter's body to get one of his water bottles. Her chest pressed into his. Then she sat up and said something that made Hunter's ears prick.

"No!" Xena clutched her heart. "Don't do this to me, Hunter."

"She got him." Mira's ears angled back. "Why are all guys like that?"

"I don't know." Shandra put her hand on Xena's. "I'm sorry."

Xena felt like her heart had stopped. "Oh, Hunter, no—"

The statement scarcely came out of her mouth when Hunter jumped to his feet. His voice rose over the noise of the beach, silencing everyone in the vicinity. "How many times do I have to tell you? I have a girlfriend! Now get off my blanket!" He grabbed the corner of his blanket and yanked it out from under Candie. She yelped and fell face first in the sand.

"What is your problem?" Candie hopped to her feet. "You can't be serious about that little twig you posted about!"

"That 'twig' is my girlfriend so watch what you say about her!" Hunter turned his back on her, marched down the beach, and spread his blanket in another spot.

Candie whirled around, her tail bristling. She marched in the opposite direction grumbling to herself. But as she passed the lifeguard station, she yelped in pain.

But Xena didn't see what happened next. Mira had leaned on the railing, blocking her view of Candie.

"I can't believe I saw that happen!" Mira bounced on her toes. "Did you see Candie's face?"

"Look at her!" Dori glared in Candie's direction. "She's faking to the lifeguard like she hurt her leg when Hunter tossed her. Doesn't look like he's buying it, though."

"Mark my words, though." Mira put her hand on her hip. "He'll end up taking her back to headquarters for 'treatment.' Yup! There they go!"

"Tramp." Shandra sniffed.

"I hope nobody drowns while he's away." Katie put a finger on her chin.

Mira gaped at her. "That's kind of morbid, Katie."

"One thing's for certain." Shandra smirked at Xena. "Hunter sure likes his girlfriend, whoever she is."

Xena turned to watch Hunter lying in the sun alone. Her chest felt full to exploding. "Can you all excuse me for a moment?" She darted down the Boardwalk, jumped down the stairs, and rushed toward Hunter. She took a moment to compose herself before tapping his shoulder.

"I said I have a girlfriend." Hunter bared his teeth. "Can't you take a hint?" He jerked off his sunglasses and froze when he saw her. "Oh."

"Hi, Hunter." Xena put her hands behind her back.

Hunter shot up to a seated position. "Xena!" He took out his earbuds while looking up and down the beach. "How long were you standing there?"

"Not long." Xena knelt on his blanket.

"That's good." Hunter exhaled a breath. "Nice suit." His eyes traced her up and down.

"Kathra picked it out for me."

"She's got good taste." Hunter drew up a knee and rested his arm on it. "What are you doing here? I thought you were hanging out with your friends."

"I am." Xena pointed to Mira and the others. "They're on the Boardwalk."

"'Sup?" Hunter called out to them and waved. They waved back, even though they probably didn't hear him.

"I came over to say hi, since I saw you here." Xena sat back on her feet.

"In that case, hi." Hunter leaned closer to her.

"Hi." Xena giggled. "I'm going to go back now."

"I'll call you later, okay?"

"Sure, but if I don't pick up it's because my phone's in the car, so . . ."

"I'll keep that in mind." Hunter gave her a half-smile that made him look even cuter than before.

Xena started to stand but after a pause, she leaned forward and gave him a peck on the cheek.

"Not that I mind, but what was that for?" Hunter grinned. "I'll do it more often."

Xena bit her bottom lip. "Mmmm . . . cause I like ya." She stood. "And because I think you're a good guy."

A real smile spread over Hunter's lips. "Thanks."

"Okay . . . bye." Xena backed away from him before turning to trot back to the Boardwalk.

"Wow." Katie examined Xena up and down as she walked up. "You two really have a thing going."

"And you still have his attention. Look. He's still watching you." Mira jerked a thumb over her shook.

Xena turned. Hunter was staring at her. He waved. "I think I'll keep him," she said.

Shandra stood. "I suppose I could learn a thing or two from you on how to handle boys." She headed down the Boardwalk followed by Katie, Mira, and Dori.

"I don't think it has anything to do with handling him." Xena waved at him over her shoulder before following after her new friends. "Hunter's great all on his own."

CONVERSATING

Hunter watched Xena rejoin her friends on the Boardwalk. She waved at him then disappeared with them in the crowd.

"A good guy, huh?" Hunter sighed, letting his hand drop. "If only you knew, Z."

With a grunt, he lay back down on his blanket and replaced his sunglasses and earbuds. The buds played a soft, lilting song that blocked out the sound of people talking, seagulls squawking, and girls screaming in the ocean. But he had set them to let in the rush of the waves crashing against the shore.

"Sorry about that," he said. "We keep getting interrupted."

Hunter didn't know what to call what he was doing. The term 'praying' seemed too cheesy and reminded him either of stuck-up, judgmental, religious types or the people back in Expermia who threw themselves in front of statues. Hunter, however, didn't consider himself like either of those.

On the other hand, if he described what he was literally doing—that is, talking to someone he couldn't see and whom he only heard in his mind's ear—he'd sound insane. So until he could come up with a better term, he called what he did Conversating, with a capital 'C.' If anyone asked, he was Conversating. If they asked with whom, he would say with someone he had known when he was young and whom he had recently reacquainted with.

"So . . . yeah." Hunter settled himself onto his blanket. "You need to make girls stop doing things like that. Candie, for instance. She's so hot, I know I'd have a good time with her, but the way I feel about Xena goes deeper than that, you know?"

"I know," said the Voice.

"I'm trying to be good here, and I'm trying to stop doing the things you don't want me to do. So why do you let girls do that?" Hunter gazed up at the sky. "She practically stuck her chest in my face. And I do so like a good chest in my face . . ." He trailed off, a grin slipping onto his face.

"Hairo!" The Voice jolted Hunter out of his thoughts.

With an effort, Hunter dismissed the image he had been courting from his mind. "Sorry, but that's what I mean. When those sort of ideas get into my head, I want to go do them. But I know that Xena's not that kind of girl, and she trusts me. I don't want to hurt her—especially not by messing with someone else. In the end I wind up so frustrated."

The Voice sighed. It seemed so close that it could have been sitting next to him. Hunter peeked out of the corner of his eye. For a moment, he saw a white German Shepherd sitting beside him. Somehow he knew that if the Voice had manifested itself into physical form then that is how he would look. But the vision passed, and Hunter found himself looking at a stretch of beach.

"I know it's hard, but this world will constantly test and tempt you. But here's the thing, Hairo . . ." The Voice sounded like it was smiling. "I am not condemning you for being tempted. You have come so far from where you used to be."

Hunter felt his heart lift so much so he almost felt as if he had left the ground. "Really?"

"And as you grow you will be able to stand no matter what comes your way."

"But what if I don't stand? What if I fall?" Hunter pictured Xena's face as it would be if he had ever cheated on her. The face he imagined—with all its disappointment, sadness, and anger—set his heart quivering. "I don't think I could take that. I don't want to be stronger; I just don't want to hurt Xena."

"Hairo." Hunter felt almost as if a heavy hand had been laid on his shoulder. "You need to learn how to stand. You need to grow and mature."

Hunter rested his arm over his eyes. The prospect of having to resist more of Candie's . . . or anyone's . . . advances left his soul feeling tired. He bit his lips together. It was funny . . . if this had happened a year ago, he probably would have tried to play both Candie and Xena for as long as possible before one or the other found out about it. But now, he couldn't stand the thought of doing that.

"You know, it's amazing how one girl could change me so much," Hunter said.

"She's not what made you change. You turned to me before you met her. That's what caused the change. You could not have met Xena until after you had grown, and your experiences helped her get through a rough time."

"So my failings and rebellion weren't for nothing."

"Of course not. I wouldn't waste the lessons you've learned and the things you've gone through."

"But what if I fail you again?"

"I won't ever abandon you."

Hunter let the grin grow on his face. Good to know. But what about Xena? Would she stick with him? Hunter couldn't handle it if she abandoned him. From the moment he met her, she made him feel wanted . . . like he had come home. He didn't want to do anything to harm her.

"You did a good job on Xena, by the way," Hunter turned to the Voice, but he couldn't see it. "She's not what everyone would call pretty, but I love everything about her. She's sweet and kind, and . . ." He paused, one ear pointing. "And she confuses me."

"How so?"

Hunter tapped his foot on the blanket. "There are sometimes when I see her where I want to hold her and protect her from everything. I want to *be* with her . . . and I'm not talking about just physically. I want *her*, if you understand. Then the next minute, I think, 'Man, I'm too young to be thinking about that kind of stuff.' I'm only sixteen. Thinking about that sort of commitment to one person for the rest of my life scares me to death—even if it is with someone as great as Z."

"It's because you are Expermian."

"What's that got to do with it?"

"If you had grown up and lived in Expermia, you would be expected to choose your mate, have a stable job and house to support her, and marry her by the time you both turned eighteen. You were exposed to that sort of thinking during your childhood.

However, you spend your formative teenage years in a country where most people don't think about marriage until their twenties. That's when they *start* looking for someone to settle down with. So you are stuck in the middle of two trains of thought."

"Fantastic . . . one more legacy Expermia has burdened me with." Hunter took a deep breath and let it out in a hiss. "I wonder how Xena feels about me, though. Do you think she's as confused as I am?"

The Voice said nothing.

Hunter let his ears tilt back. "Don't you know how she feels about me?"

"Of course."

"Are you going to tell me?"

"No."

"Why not?"

"You wouldn't want to know that."

"Yes, I do."

"No, you don't. Trust me."

Hunter crossed his arms. "Alright. Alright." His tail had fallen asleep, so he shifted it to his other side and let his eyes wander. They landed on the boardwalk where Xena disappeared with her friends. Good thing he had gotten rid of Candie when he did. He didn't want Xena to see him talking to her.

"Why is that?" the Voice said.

Long ago Hunter had learned not to be surprised when the Voice responded to his thoughts. "Girls get real jealous when they see me talking to another girl, even when I'm not doing anything. If Xena saw me talking to a knockout like Candie, she'd never give me a chance to explain."

The Voice roared with laughter. "Hairo, you have a lot to learn!"

"What's that supposed to mean?"

The Voice didn't respond but hissed in laughter.

His laugh was so infectious that Hunter found himself chuckling. "Okay, okay. By the way, thank you for letting me meet her—Xena, I mean. I don't know if I ever thanked you for it. I think . . . she makes me want to be a better person." He dug his feet in the sand. "I don't know if I do the same for her, though. Sometimes, I wonder if I drag her down."

"Hairo, I'm not just out for your good; I'm out for hers too. I won't let you get away with hurting her."

"Thank you." Hunter paused. "Did I just say thank you for promising to punish me if I mess up?"

"You did."

"Isn't that crazy?" Hunter crossed on leg over the other. "Following you is not easy. I'm doing things and being a person I would have never dreamed of being on my own."

"Didn't I warn you?"

"Yes, you did." Hunter looked at the spot where he saw the vision of the German Shepherd before. Once again, the Voice manifested itself and turned to Hunter, with eyes that Hunter could not hold. "Thanks for coming after me all that time. I feel like I found purpose in my life."

"You're welcome, Hairo," the Voice said. "It was my pleasure."

MY LITTLE HEROINE

Kathra wandered out of the Burger Shack, down the Boulevard, and onto the beach. Her new friend, Khendera, hadn't cleaned her room. So in a display embarrassing enough to cause permanent emotional trauma, her mother had marched into the Shack and had carted her off to do so. That meant that Kathra had been left on her own. But she still had half-an-hour left until she met Xena for lunch.

Kathra gazed at the blue ocean water and the sun sparkling off of it. It looked so cool and clean. A quick dip would be nice. But if she went in, she'd have to shampoo the salt out of her fur. And she had yet to find a replacement for the brand of fur shampoo she usually used—a unique blend of cleaner and conditioner that always made her fur turn out perfectly. Apparently they only carried it in the stores around New Jelu and Justin's Ridge. Without her normal shampoo, Kathra would have to do a full body conditioning and then she'd have to brush all her fur out. And she hadn't even considered what would happen if she got her hair wet. Perhaps a swim was too much trouble today.

"Thanks for coming after me all that time." Hunter's voice came to her.

Kathra swung around. Hunter lay out on a blanket on the sand, but . . . he was talking to someone. She glanced up and down the beach. No one gave him more than a passing glance, though some of the more desperate girls sighed at him as they passed. Kathra snorted. Didn't they know he was her sister's boyfriend?

"Hey, Hunter." Kathra stood in his sun so her shadow fell over him.

Hunter didn't answer her at first. He opened one eye, and then jumped a bit.

"'Sup, Kat?" Hunter moved the earbuds out of his ears. "Sorry, I didn't hear you." He sat up and moved his sunglasses to his head.

"Who were you talking to?" Kathra set her beach bag on his blanket.

"I was Conversating, but I'm done now."

"Conversating?" Kathra gave a little pout. "That's not a word."

"It is to me." Hunter patted the blanket next to him.

Kathra sat on the blanket next to him. "Fine then. Who were you *Conversating* with?"

"An old friend of mine." Hunter used a hand to shake sand out of his hair. "What are you doing here?"

"Waiting for Xena." Kathra put her hands around her knees. "My friend had to go home."

"I saw Xena earlier. She went off with Mira and her friends." Hunter buried his feet in the sand. "Why don't you call her? Oh, right! She said she left her phone in the car."

"Even if she didn't, I wouldn't call her."

"Why not?"

Kathra scooped up some sand. "Xena is finally hanging out with friends." She let the sand drain through her fingers. "She could never do that back home, but she used to let me hang out with my friends even when she was lonely. I figure I can return the favor."

"That's what I like about you two." Hunter took the sunglasses off his head. "You always take care of each other."

"Xena takes care of me, but I always get in the way."

"That's not true." Hunter tucked the sunglasses in his blanket.

"Yes, it is." Kathra used her finger to draw patterns in the sand. "She always looks out for me, but I'm a big brat. Sometimes I wish I could do something great like Xena can. She's even got all those cool Silver Fox powers—"

"Abilities," Hunter corrected.

Kathra ignored him. "I want to do something that Xena can't

for once."

"What about that medical scanner stuff?" Hunter motioned to her purse. "That's pretty cool."

"Anyone could do that if they spent the time to learn." Kathra clutched the strap to her purse. Even he knew that she didn't go anywhere without her scanner. "I want to do something that only I can do." She rested her chin on her palm.

"I see," Hunter leaned back on his elbows. "You know my friend I was talking to . . ."

"What friend? I didn't see anybody."

Hunter merely cast a look in her direction before continuing, "He once told me that everyone's given talents and abilities—some people more, some less. You have to do the best you can with what you have. Then you can fulfill the purpose you were made to fill."

Kathra let her ears fall back. "Thanks for the lesson, preacher boy."

"Preacher boy?" Hunter chuckled. "Never been called that before."

A girl ran past them. Soon another girl, then a guy ran past in the same direction. Kathra looked after them. A crowd had gathered on the water's edge.

"What's going on over there?" Hunter got to his feet.

Kathra also stood. "Can we go see?"

"Sure." Hunter jogged off in that direction. Kathra scampered after him. When they reached the edge of the crowd, he took her hand and shouldered his way to the edge of the water. Xena, Mira, and their friends stood on the shore. Mira was on the phone, her face hard.

Xena waved her hands and shouted at the crowd. "Don't stand there! Somebody, do something!"

"Xena, what's going on?" Hunter rushed to her side.

"Someone's drowning, Hunter!" Xena clasped his shoulders. "I can't get in the water because . . . my fur . . ."

Kathra scanned the horizon. A white dot far out at sea broke up the dark blue ocean.

"Where's the lifeguard?" Hunter surveyed the beach.

"I think he took Candie back to headquarters or something. She said she hurt her leg." Xena clenched her hands together. "I don't think he came back yet."

One of Xena's friends, a raccoon, thrust her nose in the air.

"Didn't I tell you?"

"That tramp causes trouble for everyone!" a tigress said, her whiskers stiffening.

Kathra glanced around. Everyone was in a panic.

"Hunter!" Kathra caught his arm. "Can you swim? Could you get to him?"

Hunter's eyes widened a bit. The idea that he could go out there must not have occurred to him. "There's one way to find out!" He charged into the water, snatching a boogie board from one of the kids in the ocean as he went.

"Mira!" Kathra turned to her. "Get off that phone and call an ambulance."

"Duh, Kathra!" Mira shot a glare at her as she put her hand over the receiver. "I'm on the phone with them now."

"Alright. That's taken care of." Kathra scanned the crowd. She spotted a horse that towered above everyone else. "You, clear this area and get a blanket to lay him on. And you," She pointed to a girl her age. "Get me some towels! Now!"

They all scrambled to do what she had asked.

"Come on, Hunter, come on." Xena's eyes were glued to the sea.

Kathra followed her gaze. Hunter had reached the place where they had seen the victim, but the victim had disappeared. Hunter paused a moment and then disappeared below the surface, the boogie board being the only indication of where he had been.

Kathra held her breath. Second after second ticked by, but Hunter did not emerge. "Come on, Hunter."

With only a white spot showing where he crashed through the surface, Hunter heaved something brown onto the boogie board. Then he ducked his head and kicked back to the shore, a white foam trailing behind him. But his kicks were slow.

"He's too tired." Kathra scanned the crowd again. An otter in skin tight swim pants gazed out to sea. He held his hands together, trembling.

"Hey." Kathra tapped him. "Can you swim?"

"I . . . I was the regional swim champion for my school," the otter said. "But . . . but, I . . . don't do well in crowds."

"This is no time for nerves!" Kathra pointed to the water. "Go out there and help him. If he gets too tired, they'll both drown."

The otter stared at her a second. Then he nodded, took a deep breath, and dashed out into the waves. He joined Hunter in a matter of seconds. Together, they pushed the board back to shore.

A brown mass of wet fur lay limp on the board. He was a brown squirrel wearing a white toga. The sides of the toga had been left open to allow flaps of skin to catch the air. He was a flying squirrel. Kathra had never seen one before.

She caught him under his arms and dragged him onto the blanket. The crowd fell in around her. "Give me some space!"

"Alright!" The horse shooed the crowd back. "Back up. Give some room." He shoved them off into a wide circle.

"Is he okay?" Xena said to Hunter.

Hunter panted, his hands on his knees. "He passed out when we were bringing him back in."

Kathra laid a finger under the squirrel's nose. Nothing. She pulled her scanner from her purse. After a quick scan, she found his heartbeat irregular and his blood oxygen level dropping. "Xena!"

Her sister knelt at her side in a moment. "Yes, Kat?"

"His heart is not beating right." Kathra whispered. "According to my scanner it's ventricular fibrillation. So, I want you to give him a little shock."

"What?" All Xena's fur stood on end. Kathra saw a little spark fly off of it, but it disappeared. "But, Kat, I can't . . ."

"It's okay." Kathra caught Xena's hand. Happily, Xena had gotten control of her electricity. "You'll be acting like a defibrillator. The shock will reset his heart and make it beat right again."

"But . . ."

"No one around here knows what you're going to do," Kathra said. "It'll be fine."

Hunter knelt next to her. "It's okay, Z. I'll tell you what to do. I won't let you hurt him."

"Please, Xena." Kathra looked her sister in the eyes. "His life is at stake."

Xena nodded.

"I'll tell you when." Kathra opened the squirrel's mouth and blew into it. When that was done, she raised her hands. She nodded at Xena.

Xena laid her hands on his chest and squeezed her eyes shut. Hunter whispered instructions into her ear. The squirrel's body jumped as electricity shot through him.

"What's going on? What's happening?" The crowd started to push forward

"Back it up! Come on!" The horse shoved them back.

Kathra consulted her scanners again. His heart beat again, but that wouldn't matter if he didn't start to breathe. She blew into his mouth again and watched his chest rise and fall. She did it again. And again.

Out of the corner of her eyes, Kathra saw the crowd grow. As more people joined in to see what had happened, even adults started showing up. Kathra felt her chest tighten.

She forced her attention back to her patient. She couldn't give into useless panic—not with someone's life on the line.

With a sharp gasp, the squirrel shot up, knocking his head with Kathra's. He coughed, spewing salt water onto the blanket. He doubled over, threw up, and then hacked again, coughing and gasping and wheezing as if he were trying to disengage his lung. A cheer rose up from the crowd. Xena threw her arms around Hunter. The otter jumped around in a circle. But Kathra kept her eyes on the squirrel. His eyes were wide, and his fur stood on end. His breathing remained shallow and quick. Panic, pure and simple.

"Hey, relax! Calm down." Kathra gripped his shoulders. "You're alright now."

The squirrel took quick, shallow breaths that made his whole body shudder. He hacked again. "Am I dead?" His voice was hoarse.

Kathra smiled at him. "You're alive."

"You're right." The squirrel coughed though this one didn't sound as painful. "If I was dead, I wouldn't be hurting so much."

"Don't talk." Kathra tried to get him to lie down. "An ambulance will be here soon."

"I thought I was in Heaven when I saw you." The squirrel wheezed in a breath. "I have never seen anyone so ethereally beautiful before." He stared straight into her eyes. "Looking at you I can understand why mortals would want to worship the stars."

Kathra leaned away from him. "Um . . ."

A siren wailed. An ambulance wheeled onto the beach.

"Out of the way." The horse pushed everyone aside so that the ambulance could park. "Here they come."

"And it's about time." Mira consulted her phone. "Actually, it didn't take that long at all. I guess it seemed longer than it was."

Emergency Medical Technicians—or EMT—rushed out of the back of the ambulance. Kathra scrambled out of the way as they checked out the squirrel. They put an oxygen mask on him and loaded him in the ambulance.

"Is he going to be okay?" Kathra tried to look in to see him. "I think he was a little dazed at the end there."

"Don't worry about him." One of the EMT shut the door to the ambulance. "We'll rush him to the hospital, but he has a good chance of survival because of your quick actions. You did a good job, kid."

A smile brightened on Kathra's face.

"Kathra!" Xena threw her arms around her. "You were great!"

Hunter ruffled her hair. "He would have been a goner if it wasn't for you."

"And you saved us from a huge liability." Mira put her phone to her ear. "Oh, what a lot I have to tell Mama! When I get done, that lifeguard is so fired! And Candie will never be allowed on this island ever again."

Shandra clasped her hands together. "That would be so fabulous."

"Hey, little foxie." The horse clapped Kathra on the back, causing her to hop forward. "Quick thinking."

"Excuse me." A reporter pushed through the crowd. She had a Losierres badge on lapel. Kathra found out later that she was one of the few reporters allowed to work on the Isle. "I'd like to interview you, young lady."

Kathra tucked her tail between her legs. She ducked behind Xena and Hunter. She didn't know why she always panicked when she met strange adults in strange places.

"This is Kathra, my sister." Xena pulled Kathra from behind her. "She organized the entire rescue."

"I saw that. You're a very brave and resourceful girl." The reporter held the microphone to her. "I'm sure you'll be an inspiration to young people everywhere once your story gets out."

Kathra looked around at the crowd. Xena gave her a thumbs up.

"The Isle is meticulous about what gets reported." Hunter patted her back. "No sensitive information will get out." He motioned to Xena with his eyes.

Kathra's tail slipped from between her legs. "Okay."

"Let's set up, guys," the reporter said to her camera crew.

Xena pointed off to the side. "I'm going to stay off camera over there, but I want you to know something. You're my hero, Kat. You do things I could never dream of doing." She gave her a squeeze. "I'm so proud of you."

Kathra beamed.

TYING UP LOOSE ENDS

If Celeste had been paying attention to the channels she flipped through, she would have seen the news report of a white fox kit who had saved the life of a flying squirrel on the Isle de Losierres. She would have stopped on the channel and stared at the screen and wracked her brain until she came up with the kit's name. Then she would have alerted Max to the fact that the Silver Fox's sister was hiding on the Isle. Surely the Silver Fox wouldn't be far behind.

That is, if she had been paying attention.

But she wasn't. Instead the gray furred vixen flipped past the channel without a thought.

She fixed her attention on the wall of televisions in front of her and focused on changing each and every one of their channels. The entire room revolved around those TVs. Each one had been tuned to a specific news channel, and her husband never changed anyone of them. That way, he could get news from anywhere in the world at a moment's notice by turning on the right TV. He said it was his eyes to the world.

Celeste made it her business to change the channels so that the next time he turned on a TV, he would not be able to get the news he required. That would really cheese him off.

And that made Celeste smile.

The door handle jiggled. Celeste scrambled to turn off the TV she had been working on before her husband, Maximilian, king of Drymairad, walked in. He was a red fox with amazing blue eyes that would calm her if she let them. Celeste made sure not to look at them. He wore his usual attire . . . a suit and tie . . . and he had styled his red hair to look like an organized mess.

"There you are, Celeste." Max stood in the doorway. "I was looking for you."

"Have you?" Celeste tossed her raven hair.

"It's been two weeks, and you haven't officially greeted our new Captain of the Royal Guard." Max gestured to the door. "He will be the one in charge of our security."

Celeste sank lower in the swivel chair she sat in. "I know what the Captain of the Guard does, Max."

"Then stand up and shake hands with him," Max said. "We'll be working with him a lot from now on."

"Just like old times," the new Captain said.

Celeste swung the chair around. A leopard she had known since she had started working with Max stood in the doorway. He wore the brown and olive uniform of the Drymairadian military and Royal Guard.

Celeste frowned. "Hello, Jordan."

"How are you, Celeste?" Jordan inclined his head in a patronizing manner.

"Not good now that you're here." Celeste thrust her nose in the air. "And it's 'Your Highness' now."

"How could I have forgotten?" Jordan chuckled. "Jané does keep reminding me."

"She's here too?" Celeste crossed her arms.

"She's my assistant." Jordan grinned, showing off some yellowish teeth. "I couldn't do this job without her."

"I know how that goes." Max clapped Jordan's back. "Behind every great man, right?"

They laughed together.

Celeste swung her chair around so that her back was to them. "I want you to know, Jordan, that I had nothing to do with this appointment. I don't know what got into Max to assign you like this." She thrust her bottom lip out. "If it was up to me, you'd be out on the street."

Max rubbed his eyes with his index finger and thumb. "You can go now, Jordan."

"Yes, Sire."

Celeste heard Jordan walk out. He shut the door with a boom that echoed across the room, leaving Max and Celeste in silence. Only the sound of rain plinking on the windows and roof invaded the hush.

"What's wrong with you, Celeste?" Max broke the silence. "Ever since he got here, you've been pouting."

"You know, Max." Celeste stroked the fur on her ears. "I don't see the point of being your wife. Everything I say gets overrided anyway."

"Over*ridden*." Max approached her chair. "Have you been studying your grammar?"

Celeste glared at him. "What do it matter? Apparently everything I say are crap 'cause you doesn't take it serious. I does not want that boob around me, and Imma tell everyone who ask me about it."

Max's ears went flat. "You're speaking that way to annoy me."

"I does not know what you is talking about." Celeste turned her nose up at him.

Max ran a hand through his hair. "Celeste, I know we have had this conversation about respect before—"

"Respect?" Celeste whirled around in her chair. "Let me tell you something about *respect*. You keep saying that I'm smart and that you value my opinion, but you don't *respect* me enough to listen to them. This isn't about some stupid dress, Max. This is about our safety—yours and mine. I don't trust him!"

"Give me one reason, Celeste." Max held up a finger. "Give me one good reason why I shouldn't have appointed him."

Celeste turned her head away from him. "I have a feeling that he's up to something."

"I need more than a feeling, darling." Max caressed her shoulder. "Jordan is the most qualified individual I know. He's been with me for years, and I trust him completely."

"But I don't." Celeste looked him in his dazzling eyes. "Why are you siding with him instead of me?"

"I'm not siding with anyone, Baby." Max sat on the arm rest. "Jordan has been with me almost since the beginning." He fidgeted a bit to move his tail to a comfortable position. "He helped me come into this position, and I promised him an appointment when

I took over the country."

"So?" Celeste tucked her chin onto her chest.

"It isn't good business to betray someone who has helped you to succeed." Max paused.

Celeste turned to him when he heaved a sigh that seemed to go down to his toes. But she wasn't about to comfort him . . . not this time.

"What I need is proof." Max stood. "Get me some proof that he's up to something, and I'll listen to anything you say."

Celeste studied his face. "You don't think I'm going to find anything, do you?"

He stroked her hair. "You may not have gotten along with him when we used to work at the Complex, but I know he's loyal to me."

Celeste slapped Max's hand from off of her head. She stood so fast the chair spun. "I'll show you, Max!" She marched out the door slammed it as hard as she could.

"Ooo . . . trouble in paradise?"

Celeste swung around. A black panther stood with a smile on her lips.

"Jané." Celeste pressed her lips together. "I heard you were here. Where have you been?"

"Walking around to familiarize myself with the palace layout." Jané motioned to the building. "The place is so huge; it'll be easy to get lost. No one would find you for days."

"Just remember whose palace you're in." Celeste started to march off.

"You don't want Jordan and I here, do you, Celeste?"

Celeste crossed her arms. "What makes you say that incredibly true statement?"

"You've been all pouty since we got here." Jané ran a hand along her whiskers. "You're rather like a little kid. But maybe that's how you finally got Max to get over me and move on. He does like to feel he's in charge all the time."

The fur on Celeste's tail stood on end. "What are you talking about?"

"Come on, Celeste. You know how he is." Jané's tail swished behind her. "He always has to have the last word—"

"I meant about him getting over you." Celeste narrowed her eyes. "You two never dated."

"He didn't want it to get out, but we did." Jané inhaled through her teeth. "He did not take it well when I broke it off. I thought he'd never get over me."

"You . . . broke up with him?" Celeste felt her skin pale.

"Don't worry about a thing, Celeste. He's over me now." Jané patted Celeste's cheek. "After all he married you, didn't he?" She gave her a wink before opening the door to Max's media room. She went in and closed the door behind her.

Celeste's stomach dropped. If Jané had broken it off with Max that could mean that Max might still have feelings for her. Maybe that's why he was so insistent on bringing her here. Now that they were working together again . . . Celeste shook her head. No, no. Max would never betray her like that. But Jané . . . she was another matter. She could try to . . .

Celeste swing around and barged into the media room. He halted. Jané stood in front of Max, straightening his tie.

"What are you doing?" Celeste stomped over to them.

Jané jerked her hands away from him. "His tie was a little crooked . . ."

"Max's tie is fine!" Celeste yanked the tie from her reach.

Max gagged. "Celeste! Celeste! Choking!"

Celeste released him.

"I'm sorry, Celeste." Jané held up her hands. "Didn't think it was a big deal. Max, do you have the palace plans with you? I'd like to study them and get an idea of where the vulnerabilities are."

"I thought that's why you were walking around the palace." Celeste put her hands on her hips.

Jané's tail stiffened, but her lips smiled. "I always see these things better on paper."

Max loosened his tie. "Jordan has it." He cleared his throat.

"Thanks." Jané inclined her head to them before she left.

"Celeste, what was that all about?" Max rubbed his throat.

"You are such a jerk!" Celeste smacked his arm as hard as she could.

"Ow, Celeste! Don't walk away from me! Celeste—"

Celeste stormed out the room and slammed it for a second time that day. "I can't live like this! Jordan and Jané have to go." She only needed evidence against them. But how could she get it?

Celeste put a finger to her chin. She needed to think. And whenever she needed to think, she knew of one place she could always go.

$* * *$

Celeste stopped at the door to the Minister of Defense's office. It used to be Max's office until an obscure succession law made him king. Since being crowned, Max and the Council had not yet appointed a new Defense Minister, so the office remained unoccupied, and the door still displayed Max's name.

She ran her fingers over the letters. "M Maximilian Descarté." She let her ears tilt back as she read his name. She still didn't know what the extra "M" stood for.

"Maybe it stands for 'Makes me so mad I could spit'!" She charged in.

Caria, Max's old secretary—and the secretary for the Minister before him—was nowhere to be seen, but her tail was visible from behind her desk. She was a skunk with large hips and a tremendously fluffy, striped tail. Celeste always had to bite down the urge to stroke it. Instead she cleared her throat.

Caria's head appeared over the desk. She kept her black hair cut short. Her brown eyes widened when she saw Celeste. "Well, hello there, queenie! I haven't seen you for a day and an age." Her head disappeared behind the desk again.

"I've been busy." Celeste walked over to the desk. She couldn't get offended at Caria's blunt tone and familiar talk. She spoke to everyone that way.

"You and me both. Any word on when hubby's going to get me a new Minister of Defense? I'm doing all his work and not getting any of his pay."

"I'm afraid not, Caria." Celeste surveyed the reception area. It had been painted yellow—almost orange—and a marble receptionist desk, with two chairs facing it, stood to the left of the door. A bookshelf filled with lots of files and books sat behind Caria's desk. The door leading from the reception area to the Minister of Defense's true office remained closed as it always did when the Minister wasn't in. The windows looking in had been made of frosted glass. From here no one could see in, but inside the office anyone could see out.

Caria hefted a box onto her desk.

"What's that?" Celeste peeked into the box filled with papers.

Caria clenched her sharp teeth. "That new Captain of the Guard and his upstart assistant's been keeping me hopping doing this and that. Never mind that with no Minister of Defense, I have to keep up with his work too! Between this and that, I'm hardly in this office anymore. And I do so love this office."

Celeste nodded. She had heard that Caria had decorated this office when she first started working here. "But why are they ordering you around, Caria?"

"Minister of Defense is supposed to be the Captain's boss, but no Minister means the Captain's my boss instead." Caria's tail bristled, making it look twice as big as before. "I hope you don't mind me saying so—"

"I couldn't stop you if I did."

"—but I don't like the looks of that new captain." Caria snorted, not even noticing that Celeste had interrupted. "Something stinks, and it's not me."

Celeste snickered. Caria didn't mind making fun of her species' stereotypes. "I feel the same way you do, Caria. I don't trust Jordan."

"Then why aren't you over at the palace complaining to Max about it?" Caria put a hand to her hip.

"Don't you think I've tried?" Celeste crossed her arms. "He won't listen to me."

"Shoot!" Caria made a sound she called "kissing her teeth"—a strange squeaking noise she made with her mouth as a sign of contempt—at least, that was what Celeste figured. "If I was as cute as you, I'd have him wrapped around my adorable tail. But I ain't one to tell you how to handle your relationships."

"Actually, there is something I want your help with . . ."

"Sorry, hon. I'd like to help you, but—" Caria patted the box. "I've got tons of work—courtesy of the Captain."

"What are those?"

"He wants me to put all these files in the record room over at the palace—his files, mind you." Caria snorted. "It's going to take me all day."

"But he can't do that, can he? This has nothing to do with palace security or national security. You're not *his* secretary."

"Don't you think I know that, girl?" Caria hefted the box. "But when I complained to dear old Maxie, he told me to just keep doing my job. He said, 'If they're up to something, don't you think

I'd figure it out?' He wouldn't listen to a word. Infuriating!"

"I know the feeling." Celeste leaned against the desk. "I was hoping you'd help me find something against Jordan and Jané. Max promised that if I did he'd make them leave."

"Did he?" Caria drummed her fingers on the box. "How 'bout I drop these off, and bring you back some coffee so we can brainstorm."

"But you have to do that, don't you?" Celeste pointed at the box. "I don't want to get you in trouble."

"He said to put them in there. He didn't say I had to file them." Caria winked. "'Sides, there's nothing I like better than booting out trash. Be back soon."

"Thank you, Caria." Celeste watched her leave. Once alone, she walked into Max's old office. The door closed behind her. She didn't bother turn on the light.

The executive desk and plump chair was just how he had left it. The walls had been painted slate gray. Two potted trees grew in the corners behind his desk. Celeste wandered around, a smile drifting to her face. Max had been so happy when he had gotten the appointment to become Minister of Defense. And he had no idea what Celeste had to go through to secure it for him . . . even though her love for him almost ruined it at the end. And it was here that she thought he had betrayed her with Gizelle only to find out that he had been trying to protect her.

"Oh, Max." Celeste lay down on top of the desk. "I won't let anything happen to you . . . even if you are so stubborn sometimes." She laid her arm over her eyes.

The door to the office lobby area opened. Celeste sat up. Was Caria back already? Through the windows, Celeste saw two figures—Jordan and Jané. She furrowed her brows. What were they doing here? She hopped off the desk. They might have run of the palace, but this area was off-limits. Jordan may have received the Captain of the Guard appointment, but that didn't give him the right to take over Max's old office.

Celeste watched them through the window. They stood close to each other, speaking with an intense look. "I wonder what they're talking about?" She opened the door a crack.

"—you sure?" Jordan had been in the middle of the sentence when Celeste opened the door.

"I told you. I sent that nosey secretary away for the day." Jane raised her hands. "We have free reign of this space. Plus, the Council's on recess, and there's a staff meeting going on for most of the day. This whole wing is deserted."

"But the cameras—"

"Max is so paranoid, he had the cameras in this office disabled a long time ago." Jané chuckled. "I guess he didn't want anyone to know what he was doing in here, and since he was Minister of Defense, no one even noticed."

"Okay, fine," Jordan said. "So what did you want to talk about?"

"I want you to take Max out at the end of the week," Jané said.

Every hair on Celeste's body rose. Did she hear that right?

"But I got my appointment two weeks ago. I'm the Captain of the Guard," Jordan said. "Won't they suspect me?"

"I had a brainstorm last night." Jané walked around the room. Celeste ducked behind the door. It wasn't opened that much, but she didn't want to take the chance that they would notice her. "We take out Max and blame Celeste for it. A crime of passion. Doesn't that sound delish? That way she'll pay for getting in my way."

"I don't think anyone will go for it." Jordan crossed his arms.

"And that's why I'm here." Jané stroked the fur on his bulging biceps. "You see, you don't pay attention to what people say. It's all over the palace about how much she hates us. And it's documented that Max and Celeste argue regularly. I hear the dispute they had about their wedding plans had the whole palace on edge for weeks."

"It's also all over the palace that she loves him with a passion."

"And we'll use that against her. I've already laid the groundwork for it. I told her that Max and I used to date, and you should have seen how jealous she got." Jané rubbed her hands together. "She's so easily manipulated. I wonder why Max fell for a ditz like that. Celeste will rue the day she interfered with *my* plans."

Celeste bit her bottom lip. Her plans? What plans?

"I can get behind that." Jordan clenched his teeth, making the vein in his neck bulge. "Ever since Max made her his personal assistant, she's been undercutting me, and he's been denying me everything I worked for. But with both of them out of the way, MFP will be mine!"

"You're thinking too small, Jordan." Jané stalked around the room. "You could be king."

King? Celeste gave a snort. Jordan could never be king, the moron.

"Me?" Jordan gestured to himself.

"Why not?" Jané caressed his cheek. "You're bigger, stronger, and with me by your side, smarter. Don't you want the benefits of everything you worked for? Now, I've got it all planned out. When we're finished, you'll be the most powerful man in the world. And me?" Her face darkened. "I'll make sure Celeste watches as I take everything she ever held dear from her."

Celeste clenched her teeth. The treachery . . . the unmitigated treachery! She nearly screamed with outrage. As a matter of fact, she did. A high-pitched screech slipped out of her mouth before she could clamp it shut.

"What was that?" Jané swung around. Her eyes darted all over.

Celeste let the door close as silently as she could before scanning the office. She had to hide. She had to hide fast! The door handle turned. Celeste skirted the desk and dove under it before the lights flipped on. Jané walked in, looking around. Happily Max favored executive style desks. The front came down to the ground so that no one could see her hiding unless they came around to the back.

"You're paranoid, Jané." Jordan strode in. Celeste heard his footsteps. "There's no one here."

"I know I heard something." Jané kept wandering around the room.

Celeste clenched her teeth together. If they found her here, she was dead. And so was Max. She had to warn him somehow. She carefully removed her cell phone from her pocket. She'd call Max. He'd come get her. But what to say to make him come? As soon as she spoke, Jordan and Jané would hear. Besides, he wouldn't believe her anyway. But what about Caria? Maybe Celeste could contact her somehow . . . but how to get a message out . . . ?

Duh! Texting! Celeste tapped a message on her phone. "Jordan and Jane r here. Get hello. Want to kick Mac." She sent it without checking it. He held her phone to her chest and hoped Caria would hurry!

In a few seconds her phone chimed. Celeste froze. Luckily she had been holding it against her chest so the sound had been muffled. With any luck the two traitors hadn't heard . . .

"There!" Jané said. "Don't tell me you didn't hear that!"

"Where did it come from?" Jordan said.

Crap! Celeste scrambled with her phone. Caria had replied, "I think autocorrect got you girl. LOL!"

Celeste clenched her teeth. She'd have to risk it. She'd have to call. Come on, Caria. Pick up. Pick UP!

"On my way now, queenie." Caria's voice boomed loud over the speaker. "Now what were you trying to say?"

"There!" Jané's heels marched over to the desk.

"Caria, listen to me." Celeste spoke as softly as she could.

"What?" Caria's voice rose even louder. "Speak up, girl!"

Jané's fingers curled around Celeste's arms. She yanked her out from behind the desk.

"Let me go, Jané!" Celeste screamed at the top of her lungs. "I will never let you get away with murdering my Maxie and framing me for it!"

"Give me that!" Jané wrenched the phone from her hands. "Who is this? Hello? Hello?" She snorted. "Hung up."

Hung up? Celeste felt a wave of shivers run up her spine. What if Caria didn't get the message?

Jordan grunted. "Who was it?"

Jané thrust Celeste into Jordan's hand before rifling through her phone. "It was that blasted secretary! She might have heard everything Celeste said."

Celeste squeezed her eyes shut and wished that to be true.

"Then what do we do?" Jordan gripped Celeste's shoulders. "She'll tell Max."

"If he believes her." Jané paced the office. "Let me think for a moment."

"I say we off Celeste right now." Jordan pulled his gun from his holster.

Celeste cringed away from him. A whimper escaped her.

"Wait!" Jané pushed his hand down. "We don't know what or if she heard anything. We might need Celeste as a bargaining chip."

"But she knows what we're planning. We can't let her get away."

"I know." Jané crossed her arms. "Let me think for a moment." She hopped onto the desk and crossed her legs. Her brows furrowed in thought.

Celeste glanced at the door. Maybe Caria did hear everything and had headed off to alert Max. And maybe she hadn't. But there was the chance. If that was the case, she had to buy them some time to rescue her. In either case, she couldn't let Jané have a chance to think.

"Jordan." Celeste turned her head so she could see him out of the corner of her eyes. "Why are you doing this? Max thinks the world of you. He . . . he wouldn't even listen to me about you."

"Good." Jané smirked. "That's how I planned it."

"Are you going to let her answer for you all the time?" Celeste squirmed in his grasp. "Max trusts you, Jordan. You're a dirty animal for betraying him like this!"

"Me betray him!" Jordan shook Celeste so hard that her head started to hurt. "Who's been slaving to stuff Max's pockets? Who's been doing all the dirty work for Max while he gets the glory? Why should Max get it all? I'm bigger; I'm stronger--"

"But you're certainly not smarter," Celeste muttered.

Jané snickered.

"Jané!" Jordan said.

"Sorry, but it's true. You are no genius, Jordan." Jané straightened his hair. "But it's okay. That's why I'm here."

"I see it now." Celeste glared at Jané. "You don't even want to be king, do you, Jordan? It's all her."

"Of course he does." Jané chuckled. "And I know what you're doing, Celeste. I've studied the palace plans thoroughly. I know how long it takes to get from the palace over to here. We'll be long gone before then."

"And you'll be criminals by then." Celeste glared at Jordan. "Is that what you want, Jordan? To always be on the run? You'll never get run of the company that way."

Jordan snorted but he said nothing.

"If you let me go, I can put you in charge of MFP. The Complex can be yours." It was a crazy lie, but Celeste didn't think she had another choice. She had to stall.

"Y—You can?" Jordan's ears stood on end.

"Jordan, you can't be serious!" Jané stood to her feet.

Wait! That worked? Celeste seized her opportunity. "I'll talk to Max about it. If you want it, it's yours."

"Shut your mouth." Jané smacked Celeste across the face. "When Jordan's king he'll have everything he wants."

"Why do you let her speak for you? You can't become king this way. The succession laws are very clear. You—" Celeste froze. She had a sudden thought. "You don't even care about Jordan becoming king, do you, Jané?"

Jané stiffened. Her ears went flat.

"You don't want to murder Max." Celeste clenched her teeth. "You're trying to get me out of the way!"

A growl issued out of Jané's throat. "Don't listen to her, Jordan."

"Jordan, wake up!" Celeste tried to turn to Jordan. He grip had tightened on her arm. "I wouldn't be surprised if this was a plan to get rid of both of us so she can have a crack at Max herself."

"That's it!" Jané removed a laser pistol from her waist. "I'm going to off her now! I'll figure out another way to make this work."

Celeste gasped. Using Jordan as an anchor, she kicked up and knocked the gun out of Jané's hands. She stomped on Jordan's foot with her high heel as hard as she could. He roared in pain and loosened his grip. Celeste wrenched her arms free.

"Get her!" Jané charged after her.

Celeste dashed out of the door and shot down the hall. She had to get to a place where she could get some help. She charged down the hall as fast as she could, darted through one of the Minister's aide's offices, and flung open the door to the other side.

Two footsteps charged after her—Jané's faster than Jordan. She always was the quicker of the two. Celeste slid around the corner and forced herself to go faster. Her lungs burned. She had to get to Max and convince him to believe her. She had to—

Two hands yanked at her tail, causing her feet to fly out from under her. She crashed onto her nose.

"I got her!" Jané pulled her by the tail. "Jordan, stop lagging! Get her!"

Celeste screamed. She wiggled onto her back and kicked Jané in the nose, but unlike Jordan, Jané didn't let go. Rather, she reached up to grab her waist.

"Jordan!" Jané shouted. "Get—" She made a gurgling noise that sounded familiar to Celeste—the same kind of sound King Fredelep made the day he was assassinated. Jané's entire weight collapsed on top of Celeste.

Celeste rolled Jané off of her. Blood seeped out of a wound in her back. It spread unto the floor where she lay dead.

"What the—?" Celeste stood, nearly slipping in Jané's blood.

"Celeste!" Jordan's voice echoed down the hall. He walked over to her, gun in hand.

"Get away from me!" Celeste tried to run, but slipped again. Jordan caught her arm before she fell.

"Relax." Jordan set her on her feet. "You're safe now."

Celeste tried to jerk her arm away but he held it fast. "You tried to kill me!"

"Do you think I would do something like that just because we don't like each other?" Jordan narrowed his eyes. "Protecting you is my job, though you nearly messed up everything. She was the one planning to get you and Max, not me. I was trying to get evidence against her when you showed up."

Celeste ears fell. Her gaze dropped to Jané. "But I—I thought that you were . . ."

"That you were as stupid as you look?" Max's voice rang through the air.

Celeste whirled around. "Maxie!"

Max stood down the hall. Celeste spied Caria peeking at the scene from around the corner behind him.

"Let her go, Jordan." Max pointed his gun at him.

Jordan held up the hand he held the gun with but kept firm hold on Celeste. "Max, let me explain—"

"Explain what?" Max's tail bristled. "That you betrayed me? That you were planning on murdering me?"

Jordan chuckled. "It was all an act, Max."

"If it was an act, let her go!" Max said.

Jordan didn't move. "Max . . ."

"Don't try to con me with your stories. I turned on the cameras in my office, Jordan. I saw myself what you were planning—that you had a gun to Celeste's head." Max flared his nostrils. "You are in deep. Now I'm giving you one last chance. Let her go, and I'll *think* about being merciful."

Jordan jerked Celeste closer to him. "You think you have everything figured out, do you? But I still have her." He put his gun to her head. "If you want her alive, drop your weapon."

Max clenched his teeth. "You can't get out of this, Jordan."

"I guess you don't want her to survive this," Jordan said. Celeste heard his gun charge.

Celeste squealed. "Maxie . . ."

"Alright, Jordan, alright. I'm dropping it." The gun clanked to the ground. "Don't hurt her."

"You really do love her." Celeste felt Jordan grin. His breath was hot in her ear. "I guess it wasn't an act you and J.R. put on at your wedding. Now slide it over."

Max shoved the gun across the floor with his toe.

"Now, Celeste, pick it up." Jordan shoved his gun in Celeste's neck.

She bent over to pick it up, feeling Jordan bend with her. The gun never left her neck.

"Point it at Max."

Celeste's ears twitched. She must have heard that wrong. "What?"

"Nothing would be sweeter than watching my nemesis being gunned down by his own wife." Jordan roared with laughter.

"If you think I'm going to shoot Max, you're crazy!" Celeste snarled.

"If you don't, I'll shoot you and then use you as a shield while I get him." Jordan pressed the gun into her neck. "It's either him or both of you. Your decision. On three . . . one . . ."

"Don't do it, queenie!" Caria called from her hiding spot. "He'll shoot you afterward!"

"Shut up!" Jordan leaned close to Celeste. "I'm not going to hurt you. On the contrary, I'll need some kind of bargaining tool to get me out of this mess, *queenie*. Two . . ."

Celeste turned her attention to Max. His eyes roved the hallway around them, obviously trying to look for something to save both their lives. Her eyes stung, but she knew that there was only one thing left to do. She lifted the gun and pointed it at Max. "I'm sorry, Maxie."

His eyes locked onto her. After swallowing hard, he said, "It's okay, Baby."

Seeing Max's face made Celeste want to curl up and sob. But she had already decided what she must do. No turning back. Besides, in a choice between Max's life and hers, there was no contest.

"Three."

Celeste pitched her head to the side, and used the momentum to swing around, while squeezing the trigger. She knew that firing that gun sealed her fate. She couldn't take out Jordan like this. He'd gun her down in the next second. But at least she could slow him down . . . enough for Max to get him.

She only hoped that Max would be alright without her . . . he had to be. He had intelligence and charisma. No one else on the planet had his bravery. He might even find another wife to love him someday. No, he'd be fine. But her, on the other hand . . .

She hoped that being shot didn't hurt too much. If it did, she hoped that she would be dead before she felt anything. And she hoped that Max was right and that there was no Hell. But if he was wrong she hoped that she had been good enough to make it into Heaven. She should be. After all, she was giving her life for the one person she loved in the world. That should counteract all the bad things she'd done, right? . . . tip the scales in her favor, so to speak.

All this passed through her mind in a moment. Jordan's howling in pain as her shot penetrated his leg snapped her out of it. Celeste hit the floor with a thud and covered her head with her hands.

Two hands enveloped her. She felt her head being pressed against a muscular chest.

"It's okay, Celeste. It's over now." Max's voice came to her. "I'm here."

Celeste dared to open her eyes. Max held her close, and Jordan lay in a pool of blood, a wound in his chest. But she was alive. She was alive! The realization hit her like a vehicle traveling at supersonic speeds in a high-speed transport tunnel.

"Oh, Max!" She clung to his shirt. Tears streamed down her face, and she wailed so hard that her throat hurt. "I thought I was going to die!"

"I know, baby, I know. I'm here now." Max glared at something behind him. "Why didn't you take the shot before?"

"Sorry, sir." A guard walked up to Celeste. "We couldn't get a clear shot until she pitched her head like that."

Max held Celeste tighter. "Sweetheart, I'm so sorry. I should have listened to you. If Caria hadn't convinced me to turn on those cameras in the office, he could have . . ."

"Don't say it." Celeste trembled all over.

Max helped her to her feet. "Let's get you out of here."

"Your Majesty." Another guard walked over to them. He was a dog . . . or a fox . . . a hybrid, maybe? "I understand that now isn't a good moment, but I would like to settle on a time where we can get a statement from the queen about what happened."

"What do you mean what happened?" Max shouted. All his fur

stood on end. "You saw what happened."

"Sire, you know the law." The guard snapped his heels together. "One of our officers discharged a weapon and shot a palace official. We need a statement for the investigation."

Celeste laid her head on Max's shoulder. Let him handle it for her. She didn't want to talk to anyone. The feel of the gun against her skin and the thought that she was going to die and wondering what would happen after filled her mind. And the thought of going to Hell sent a chill up her spine.

Her eyes fell to Jordan, laying there in his blood. He caused all this; he was the problem; he was the traitor. He tried to make her betray the one person who had ever cared for her. She clenched her teeth and glowered at him.

And then his eyes moved.

He was alive . . . but not for long, Celeste could tell. His eyes roved the area, seeking something to land on. He was probably thinking the same things she had been thinking when she thought her life was about to end: was there a Heaven, and if so was he good enough to get into it?

Celeste knew he wasn't.

And judging by the way his eyes jerked around, he knew it too. They finally landed on her, pleading as though she could do anything about his situation. They both knew that if Hell existed, he was headed there.

And if Hell did exist, Celeste saw the moment he entered it.

A smile slipped onto her face.

She picked up her head and turned to the soldier. "It's okay, Maxie. I think I can talk about this now."

GOOD FOR THE SOUL

The smile on Celeste's face worried Max.

The last time Celeste had seen someone die, she had been hysterical to the point of hospitalization. This time, too, she had begun having symptoms of hysteria but then . . . stopped. Sure, she acted concerned and scared during the interviews she had to undergo, but Max saw that smile lurking under the surface, ready to sneak onto her face when she wasn't paying attention.

It wasn't normal. Even *he* had only smiled at death once . . . maybe twice . . . but still. Celeste was in shock or something similar, Max knew it, but the doctors had cleared her. What did they know, anyway—the quacks. Max knew Celeste. She was suffering.

And she wouldn't be suffering if it hadn't been for him.

He gazed into the fire crackling in the fireplace. Rain plinked on the windows and roof. It had rained all afternoon, leaving the palace chilled. The palace had been constructed centuries ago, but until now, Max had not noticed the drafts constantly blowing through the cracks in the stone walls.

He shifted in the oversized armchair and wrapped his arms around Celeste. They had taken refuge from the chilled air in the antechamber of their bedroom, a thickly carpeted room with large windows and heavy, brown curtains. The lights had been dimmed, and Max had ordered no one to disturb them for the night. Celeste cuddled in his lap and snuggled her nose under his chin.

"Maxie." Celeste turned her big, green eyes to him. "Can I ask you a question?"

"Of course, Baby."

"Did you ever date Jané?"

"What?" Max jolted. "Of course not! Why would you even ask that?"

"I didn't think so." Celeste snuggled back in her place. "Jané told me you did, but I knew she was lying."

"Why would she say something like that?"

"She wanted to make me jealous . . . she wanted to give me a motive to attack you." Celeste took a deep breath. She spoke in a sort of sleepy tone Max only heard when she felt completely at ease. "But I think that she only wanted it to look like I was going to attack you so she could get rid of me." She chuckled to herself. "What made her think anyone could ever come between us?"

Max gaped at Celeste. The way she spoke—as if she were utterly contented—worried him. She saw two people die today.

"Celeste, are you alright?" Max tilted his head until he looked into her face. "You witnessed something horrible, yet you're acting like this is the best day of your life."

Celeste laughed so melodiously that Max almost forgot to be concerned for her. "Every night that I'm in your arms is the best night of my life."

"You know what I mean, Celeste!" Max slammed his fist on the arm rest. "If Caria hadn't convinced me to turn on those cameras and look at what was going on in there, I could have lost you." He wrapped his arm around her waist. "I couldn't bear to lose you, Celeste." He held her tighter.

"Maxie, it's okay." Celeste wormed her arms around him. "You don't need to beat yourself up. They got what was coming to them, and I'm with you now. Just chalk this up to experience. You can't trust just anybody."

"Believe it or not, that has been my mantra." Max buried his nose in the fur on her shoulder. Her smell settled the fur on the back of his neck. "There are three people in the world that I have ever dared to trust, Celeste. Jordan was one of them. I trusted him with the most important thing in my life, and he used you against me."

"Oh, Maxie, I'm sorry." Celeste stroked the fur on his arm. Between her actions and her smell, Max managed to take a breath and raise his head.

"All better?" Celeste looked at him with that innocent face that melted any resistance he had.

"I'm fine, Celeste."

"Good." Celeste settled herself in her original position. Silence fell with only the crackle of the fire and tinkling rain interrupting the hush. "Who are the other two?" she said after a while.

"Excuse me?"

"That you trust." Celeste played with the buttons on his shirt. "You said you trusted three. Who are the other two?"

"You are one." Max kissed the top of her head. "I trust you with everything."

Celeste's eyes shone. "Really, Maxie?"

"Of course."

Celeste wiggled in his lap until she sat up. Then she caught his face in her hands and stared him straight in the eyes. The gold in her eyes sparkled and danced in the firelight. "I will never betray that trust, Maxie. I promise."

Max caressed her hands. "I believe you."

"You better." Celeste pulled him into a kiss. When she pulled away, she rested her head on his chest. "And the other one?"

Max took a deep breath. He scratched his ear and said nothing.

Celeste looked up at him. "Maxie?"

"It was my best friend." Max let his ears drop.

"I didn't know you had a best friend." Celeste ran her hand up his chest. "Why haven't I met him?"

"Because 'had' is the operative word there." Max rested his elbow on the arm rest. His eyes drifted to the window where the rain cascaded down the panes in sheets.

"What happened to him?" Celeste narrowed his eyes. "Did he betray you too?"

"No." Max turned his gaze to the ornately carved ceiling. "I betrayed him."

"No way!" Celeste faced him, her eyes wide. "You would never do anything like that. I don't believe it."

Max felt a smirk come to his lips. "I betrayed the former king."

"That's different." Celeste waved her hand. "Fredelep deserved it. He was horrible." She snorted. But after a moment, she turned her eyes to Max. "So what happened between you and your ex-best friend?"

Max let his eyes close. He hadn't wanted to admit this to her, but once she got going he couldn't resist her. Why fight it? "I asked him to give me a place to do some work. When I got there I hurt his friends, burned down a building, and kidnapped some children under his care—not that I knew it at the time, mind you."

"Are you talking about that place we found the Silver Fox?"

"When he came to get them, I refused to let them go and throttled him." Max felt his ears touch the back of his head. "I felt that I could get what I wanted without giving up anything. I thought that my Silver Fox Emulator made me more powerful than he, and that he was dispensable. Little did I expect that the Silver Fox would fight back." He grunted. "I still need to find a way to counter her abilities. Until I do, I can't go after her again."

"Wait a minute!" Celeste nearly jumped to her feet. "You're talking about J.R. Dunsworth!"

Max nodded.

"But he ruined my wedding. And he destroyed your research!" Celeste frowned. "How can you be friends with a fiend like that?"

Max turned his eyes to the carpet. He couldn't bear to look at her reproachful face. "You have no idea what he had done for me, Celeste."

"Do you mean trying destroying your research, threatening me, or ruining my wedding?" Celeste counted them off on her fingers.

Max studied her. "Do you know how I got to this position, Celeste?"

"Hard work and perseverance?"

"And an insane amount of research." Max pulled her back onto his lap. "J.R. helped me with that. He used to break into buildings that used my security systems and then tell me where they were lacking so that I could come up with newer versions before anyone else could. My security was always one step ahead of criminals and the competition because of him. I have no doubt that is what he was doing when he broke into the Complex; he always returned the things he took from me. His work built my company up to the place where it is today."

"But he ruined my perfect wedding!" Celeste wailed.

"My, how you harp on that."

"I've been looking forward to that day my whole life." Celeste clenched her fists. "I never thought I would get out of slavery, much less get married. So when it finally happened, I wanted it to be the most perfect of all days. Everything was supposed to be flawless; it was supposed to be the happiest day of my life. It was the only thing I have ever had that was all mine and all about me. He ruined that!"

Max patted her face. "Try not to be too upset about that, darling. That was my fault."

"Did you tell him to ruin my wedding?"

"Of course not."

"Then how can it be your fault?"

Max squirmed in his seat. Did the conversation really have to go this way? But looking at her face, it did. She would never let this go until he gave her a proper explanation. "Ease up a second, Celeste." He patted her back.

Celeste slid out of his lap. Max walked to the bedroom, and opened the lockbox he kept in his night table drawer. From there, he removed a package filled with photographs. He sorted through the photos, putting in one pile the photos that would truly disturb Celeste and the rest in another. He gathered up the latter, removed a letter from the package and carried these back to Celeste.

"What's this?" Celeste was sitting on the arm of the chair when he came back in.

Max handed her the papers and watched her sort through the pictures that he had rifled through a million times. All of them were photos of him and Celeste—either together or apart—engaged in various activities. There were pictures there of them on their first official date, of Celeste eating breakfast in her old apartment, of Max's private research at the Complex, and of confidential meetings hosted in the palace grounds.

As she went through picture after picture, Celeste's face paled. Her eyes grew wide. "What is this? Who took these pictures?"

Max handed her the letter and watched her read the words he had memorized:

> "Max, because I once considered you a friend (an oversight on my part) I feel the need to warn you. Stay away from my girls, and I'll stay away from yours. -J.R."

When Celeste looked up, her bottom lip trembled.

"I got that after we started dating." Max cleared his throat. He voice had started to quiver. "At first, I didn't worry about it too much. J.R. isn't known to do anything without reason, and I had no reason to believe he would come after you if he said he wouldn't." He ran his hands over his ears. "But once we started getting serious, and especially after we announced our engagement, I couldn't stand the thought that he would hurt you. The threat of that was killing me, so I tried to get rid of J.R. before he could try anything."

"That's why you ordered that raid of Justin's Ridge."

"And that backfired." Max bit his lip. "Now he's loose, and I don't know where he is. I've cut him off from all help, but he doesn't need help to do what he wants to do. And now he has a reason to come after us." He shook his head. "Jordan was my attempt at keeping you safe. He knew J.R. like I did, and Jordan was stronger than both J.R. and myself." He clenched his teeth and hands and squeezed his eyes shut. "I'm trying to do everything I can to protect you, and I keep failing. I can't lose you, Celeste. I can't lose you . . . not like I lost . . . I . . ." He clenched his fists so hard that his fist started to tremble. A growl tore out of him. "Why am I so useless?" He pounded his fists against his head.

"Maxie!" Celeste leapt from off the arm rest. She caught his hands and forced them down. "Stop it, Max. You're hurting yourself."

"What do I care?" Max shouted. "I deserve it!"

"Max, please stop!" Celeste threw her arms around him and held him so hard that her veins started to show through her fur.

Max tried to jerk out of her grasp but found himself held to the spot. He had no idea she could be so strong. Perhaps he . . .

He froze. What was that? Something moved him, vibrating or trembling against him. Max stood still, his breaths coming in shallow rasps. He calmed his breathing and listened. Celeste's shoulders pitch up and down. Her body shook with the force of her sobs. Max let a groan slip out of him. Celeste was suffering again, and it was his fault.

He closed his eyes and locked his pent-up frustration back into the recesses of his mind to where it had been all those years. He couldn't let it control him now—not after so many years of discipline. "Celeste, you can let me go now."

"No!" she screamed between sobs.

"It's okay. I'm fine now."

Celeste released him, but slowly as if prepared to grab him again.

"Sorry you had to see that, Celeste." Max straightened his tie. The places where he had hit himself stung. He hoped they wouldn't develop into bruises.

"You must have been holding on to that for so long." Celeste wiped her eyes with her hands. "You must have been through something horrible. What happened?"

Max stumbled backwards. The question slammed straight into him. "I . . . I don't want to talk about it."

"Not talking about it put bruises all over your face, Max." Celeste caressed his cheeks. He winced as pain shot through him. Bruises? Fantastic. He would have to wear an image-generator to hide it in the morning.

"Max." Celeste took his hands. "Please talk to me. You said you trusted me with everything. Why not this?"

He studied her, from her hands clasping his to her pleading eyes. He turned away from her and forced the words out of his mouth. "I'm talking about my mom."

"Your mom?" Celeste's ears pricked. "You never told me about her. I thought she was dead."

"She's not . . . or at least, I have no reason to believe she is." Max stared at the carpet. "When I was seven, my father got rid of her."

"What do you mean got rid of her?"

Max's heart thundered in his chest. Nothing in him wanted to talk about this, but for Celeste . . . "My father used to beat up on her a lot. She used to do everything she could to keep it from me, but I knew. I loved my mother. I didn't want to see her hurt like that. Once he beat her so badly that she passed out, but the police wouldn't do anything about it."

"Why not?"

"I'm still trying to figure that out, Celeste." Max clenched his fists so hard his nails pierced his skin. Even now he snarled at the thought of it. "I remember thinking that they wanted to help us but something was stopping them. They told me that I was to take care of her. So one day, I did just that. I charged at that bastard and bit him so hard that I drew blood. He knocked me across the room, and I hit the wall so hard it broke my tail. I don't know if you've ever noticed, but that's why my tail is crooked."

Celeste shook her head. "I hadn't noticed."

"In any case, it made him back off."

"Good for you, Maxie!"

"I had never felt so good in my life—so empowered!" Max clenched a fist. "I knew at that moment he would never hurt my mama again."

"That's right!"

"And the next day he sold her."

Celeste voice went up an octave. "Into slavery?"

"Is there any other way?"

"That's horrible!" Celeste stomped her foot. "That's so horrible! Where is she now?"

"I don't know."

"You don't . . ." Celeste stared at him. "Then why haven't you been looking for her? You have all the resources in the world! Go find her!"

Max watched his shadow flicker on the curtains. The rain had slowed to a drizzle. "I couldn't stop my father from taking her, Celeste. I tried, but I couldn't stop him. She'll never forgive me—"

"You were seven years old, Max! That wasn't your fault. Your mom will forgive you for that. What she won't forgive is having all these resources and not even attempting to find her." Celeste's tail bristled. "How could you leave her in that life? This is the exact reason we should have abolished slavery long ago!"

"I already explained to you, Celeste, that if we abolish slavery right now, we'd end up with a bunch of people running around who don't know what to do with themselves." Max turned his eyes away from her. "Once the programs are in place to help them transition into freedom, then I'll do it."

"A lovely excuse not to implement a controversial law." Celeste put her hands on her hips. "And it doesn't explain why you haven't even tried to look for her. I don't know who is the more cruel, your father for selling her into that life or you for leaving her there. You're the king! And even before that, you and your company had rescued millions of people from slavery, including me! But you're not even trying to save your own mother!" She swung around so her back faced him.

Max reached out his hand to her. "Celeste . . ."

A grunt of disgust was her only reply.

Max drew back his hand. There may as well have been a million miles between them. The last person he had left had abandoned him. But how could he expect it to turn out differently? He deserved to be alone. "Celeste, I'm sorry. I'm truly sorry." He headed to the bedroom.

"My family died in slavery." Celeste's voice halted him. "I . . . wanted to see them again so badly. I wanted to show them this grand palace; show them what I have accomplished, but . . ." She fell silent for a moment. "If your mom's alive, we have to find her. We can look together." She looked up at him. "I know we can find her if we try."

Max gazed at her. A smile crept onto his face. He rushed to her, wrapped his arms around her, and kissed her over and over. "How did I land such a great girl like you?"

"You saved my life when you freed me from slavery, Max." Celeste nuzzled her nose under his chin. "I will love you forever for what you did."

Max eased down in the chair and let Celeste snuggle onto his lap. They sat together and listened to the fire pop and crackle. Nothing in the world could compare to this . . . no one on the planet could be better than this vixen right here on his lap. He stroked Celeste's hair and stared out of the window.

The clouds had parted, and the crescent moon shone down on them, caressing them with its silvery light. To Max, it was the sign of good things to come.

BREAKOUT

The crescent moon.

In ancient Expermia, it had been a sign of blessing and favor. Even in modern Expermia, celebration greeted a crescent moon for the people held it as a sign of the gods' approval.

That is, for those idiots who still believed in the gods.

Up until three weeks ago, Marviot had been one of those idiots, but the Outsiders' invasion of Expermia had cured him of that. If the gods couldn't stop those infidels from invading and desecrating their temples, what good were they? Marviot had spent his whole life doing what the gods wanted, and here he set, in an Outsider prison for all his efforts.

And Karalaina was in an Outsider's arms—another Outsider's arms! When Marviot got out of this prison, he would tear her away from him and rip him limb from limb. She belonged to him. One way or another, she would see that. And the Outside would regret laying his dirty paws on her.

But first he needed to escape. He refused to sit around and wait for the gods to rescue him. Both his grandmother and his father had been executed waiting for that.

And his turn loomed near.

"Hey!"

Marviot looked out of his cell without moving. Through the

bars he spied two guards, a raccoon and an ocelot both in olive and brown uniforms. The ocelot had a plate full of Outsider food. Marviot narrowed his eyes. That ocelot . . . what a strange Outsider . . . rather perfect looking. Every strand of the brown and white patches of his fur was exactly the same shade as the others—no variation. He had no blemishes and no imperfections.

"Eat up." The ocelot set the dish down and slid it through the opening.

Marviot sneered. The Outsiders wouldn't even allow him the respect of eating with utensils or the dignity of eating with other prisoners all because he had critically injured three guards and five prisoners with a fork the last time they let him into the prisoners' mess hall. No wonder they held him in the cell far away from the others.

"Come on." The ocelot guard nudged the tray through the opening with his foot. "Eat. You need to keep your strength up."

"Why?" Marviot turned up his nose. "So I can die by your filthy Outsider hands?"

"Perhaps so." The raccoon smirked.

"I'd rather starve." Marviot turned his head away from them. His hair, brown with blue at the ends, swayed with the motion. It hadn't been cut since he had been locked away. And with good reason. Even the Outsiders knew it would be stupid to put Marviot in the same room with scissors.

"He hasn't eaten anything since I've come on duty two weeks ago." The ocelot put his hands on his hips, causing his pelvis to jut out slightly. Marviot narrowed his eyes. He had seen that gesture somewhere before . . .

"He must have been eating something." The raccoon studied Marviot. "He doesn't look any thinner."

"Maybe he's been getting outside help." The ocelot stared straight at Marviot. And if Marviot didn't know better, he would say the ocelot winked at him. "He's not supposed to be having contact with anyone." He removed his keys. "Let's search his cell. Get your weapon ready."

The raccoon removed his gun, while the ocelot opened the cell door. Training his gun on Marviot, the raccoon edged in. "Keep sharp; I hear he's wily."

"You have no idea." Marviot pounced on him. He wrenched the gun away from him and struck him behind the ear. The raccoon collapsed on the floor.

Marviot pointed the gun at the second guard.

"If that's the best guards the Outsiders have to offer, it's a wonder you haven't escaped already." The ocelot turned to Marviot. "Put down that gun."

"Just checking the accuracy." Marviot raised it. "Good to see you, Cortraire. Or rather good to see the disguise you're wearing. It's excellent. I didn't have any idea it was you. You don't look like an Expermian at all."

"Let's get out of here." Cortraire glanced around. "I don't like doing this." He tossed Marviot something he pulled from his pocket. "Hurry and put that on. The cameras won't stay jammed for long."

"What is this?" Marviot studied the object. It looked like a watch. "I don't need to know what time it is."

"It's a device the Outsiders call an image-generator." Cortraire glanced up and down the hall. "It projects an image over your body like the one I have. I've already set it, so put it on."

"To think we've been reduced to this." Marviot placed it on his wrist. He morphed from fox into raccoon in seconds—even down to the ridiculous striped tail. "I'm still in my prisoner clothes."

"Apparently, the Outsiders make security and prisoner uniforms that repel image generators . . . as a security measure, I assume. Change clothes with the guard, and let's get out of here." Cortraire darted down the hall. "I'll make sure the coast is clear." He rounded the corner and disappeared.

Marviot did what he was told. But before he walked out, he looked at the Outsider in the cell. An idea popped into his head.

He stooped down and replaced the Outsider's watch with his. Then he tinkered with it. The holographic display on the watch . . . or image-generator as Cortraire called it . . . made the process of changing the projected image fairly easy. Once he selected the base image as a fox, Marviot tinkered with the ears, muzzle, and hair until the Outsider looked like a decent replica of him. Not perfect, but the Outsiders would never know the difference. Then as a final thought, he removed the image-generator off the raccoon's wrist, yanked off the straps, and forced the core component of the device down the Outsider's throat. The image of Marviot wavered a bit but held still.

Marviot stood over the figure. It had been a risk—who knew

how powerful this device was . . . or even if it would short out inside the Outsider's stomach—but the image held.

"I'm so good." Marviot grinned at his work.

"Marviot!" Cortraire's footsteps came to him. "What are you doing?"

Marviot intercepted Cortraire before he saw what Marviot had done. Cortraire had such a tender heart that he would never agree to it. He probably already feeling guilty about breaking into an Outsider jail. "Had a hiccup figuring out these Outsider clothes."

"What happened to your disguise?"

"I am not disguising myself as an Outsider." Marviot put on the guard's hat and hid his hair and his ears as best he could. "Don't worry. I got this. Let's get out of here."

Cortraire grunted. "If we get caught, Marviot, this is your fault."

"We won't get caught, Cortraire." Marviot followed him out. "The Outsiders won't even know that I'm missing."

ABOUT THE AUTHOR

M.R. Anglin is a rather private person who is the author of *Lucas, Guardian of Truth,* the self-published *Silver Foxes* series, and a number of short stories. What that specific number is, however . . .

9 7 9 8 2 0 1 5 2 2 4 1 4